THE DARK STAIRS

A HERCULEAH JONES MYSTERY

THE DARK STAIRS

BY BETSY BYARS

A TRUMPET CLUB SPECIAL EDITION

ISBN 0-590-05638-7

Copyright © 1994 by Betsy Byars.
All rights reserved. Published by
Scholastic Inc., 555 Broadway, New York, NY 10012,
by arrangement with Viking Penguin,
a division of Penguin Books USA Inc.
TRUMPET and the TRUMPET logo
are registered trademarks of Scholastic Inc.

12 11 10 9 8 7 6 5 4 3 2   7 8 9/9 0 1/0

Printed in the U.S.A.   40

First Scholastic printing, November 1996

Contents

THE DARK STAIRS

1
DEAD OAKS

Friday the thirteenth came early that year, in January, making it even more unlucky. Later Herculeah would remember, that was the day it all started. If she had been a superstitious person she would have thought there was a connection between that and the terrible events that followed.

But on that Friday Herculeah was buying a pair of binoculars. "I'm going to take these to the window and try them out, all right?" she said to the clerk.

She crossed to the plate-glass window and lifted the binoculars to her face. Her dangle earrings brushed against her cheeks as she leaned forward and focused on a rundown house across the street.

"What's my dad doing there?"

"Where?" said the clerk.

"He's at that old house across the street. At Dead Oaks."

"So?"

"So my father's a police detective. There must be something wrong."

She adjusted the binoculars again. As usual her father had on a rumpled jacket and a loose tie. He looked, not like a detective, but like a man who was lost.

"I wish they'd tear that old house down," the clerk said, "it's scary. I'd love to see a nice mini-mall over there."

"I've got to check this out," Herculeah handed the binoculars to the clerk. "Don't sell these. I'll be right back. And don't sell those granny glasses either."

Herculeah rushed out the door. "Dad!" she called. Her father pulled the iron gate shut, chained and padlocked it. He waited as she crossed the street.

"So what's wrong?" Herculeah asked.

"You tell me."

"I mean what are you doing here. What happened?"

"Nothing major."

"But what? I've always been interested in this old house."

"You're interested in everything."

"What do you expect with a cop and a private eye for parents." She grinned.

Her father shook his head as if the combination was too much for him.

"So what is the minor thing that brought you here?" she persisted.

"Oh, some of the neighbors saw a prowler. I was just checking it out."

"And?"

"And I found no signs of forced entry. I found nothing to suggest foul play. Satisfied?"

"Of course not."

Herculeah made a ponytail of her long hair and held it back with one hand. She looked beyond her father to the house.

The house was dark and foreboding. It had been named Twin Oaks for the huge trees that grew on either side of the walkway. The trees had been dead for years, and their stark black skeletons made people now call it Dead Oaks.

"Dad, you know how my hair always starts to frizzle when something's getting ready to happen?"

Her father's beeper sounded and he lifted his radio to listen. "Right," he said.

"Because, Dad, my hair's frizzling right now. Look!" She released her hair and, caught by a breeze, it floated around her.

"I'm on my way," her father said.

"This thing with my hair is automatic. It's like how animals fluff out their fur when they're in danger, so they look bigger and more threatening."

Her father looked at her. "If you get any more threatening, you're going to fly away."

"I'm serious."

"I got to go."

Herculeah watched her father get into the car. He said something to the driver and waved at Herculeah as they drove off.

Herculeah went back to the store.

"What'd you find out?"

"Nothing much. Some neighbors have reported seeing a prowler."

"I could have reported that myself," the clerk said. "I don't know why anyone would go over there. They say there's a dead body inside." She straightened. "So, do you want the binoculars or the glasses?"

"The trouble is I want them both. I need the binocs because there are a lot of things in the distance that I need to see—like at stakeouts with my mom. But those glasses . . . I tried them on, and the world disappeared in a kind of fog. It was great. I felt as if I were in a—I don't know—a think cocoon. I felt I could write whole novels and paint masterpieces and puzzle out things that bother me." She smiled. "Like what's going on over at Dead Oaks." Herculeah held out the glasses. "You want to try them?"

The clerk shook her head. "If glasses could make me think better, I'd make a beeline for LensCrafters. I'll need two dollars to hold the glasses, and three for the binoculars."

"There." Herculeah brought out a crumpled five-dollar bill and ironed it flat on the counter. "I'll probably have the rest of the money by tomorrow."

"That'll be fine."

"I could even be back today before five if my mom gets home."

Herculeah started for the door. The shop bell rang as she stepped outside. She paused for a moment, looking at the house across the street.

Built of sandstone, now darkened by moss and years, the house in a certain angle of sunlight still looked grand. But in the shadows of late afternoon, with the dead trees, it was forbidding. She remembered the clerk's words: "They say there's a dead body inside."

She felt a chill that had nothing to do with the weather, and wrapped her jacket around her.

2
A BOY NAMED MEAT

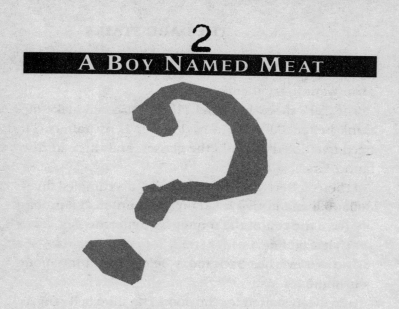

Herculeah turned the corner. She had lived on this street all her life, but now the street was beginning to go commercial. People were opening businesses in their homes.

Herculeah's mother had been the first, with her private investigator business. The small tasteful sign had gone up one night:

Mim R. Jones
Private Investigator

Within a week, another sign sprang up down the block. It was not as tasteful:

Madame Rosa
Palmist
Walk-ins Welcome

After that, the signs sprang up nightly, like mushrooms. Bernie Holden: Accounting. Bessie Youngstern: Alterations. Cheri's Cakes. One-Day Dentures. Divorces $35.00.

Herculeah liked it. She felt it gave the street a prosperous look that other residential streets didn't have.

Now she walked quickly until she came to the steps of her house. She stopped abruptly beside her mother's sign. Sitting on the steps, blocking her way, was Meat, a boy who lived across the street.

As soon as Meat saw Herculeah, he put out his arms and took hold of the metal banisters. "Don't go inside," he said.

"Well, I guess I can chat for a minute," Herculeah said. She sat on the bottom step and turned toward him. "Guess what, Meat. You know that shop Hidden Treasures? Well, I went in there to try out some binoculars—which I need for helping Mom—and I was just checking them out when I saw my father over at Dead Oaks."

"What was he doing there?"

"He wouldn't tell me. 'Nothing major'—that's what he always says."

"I hate that house," Meat said. "It gives me the creeps."

"Me too."

"My mom saw the old man that lived there one time."

"Really?"

"My mom was selling Girl Scout cookies and she went up and knocked—she was a little girl then, she might even have been a Brownie—and he came to the door, and he had a walking cane, and he lifted it like he was going to hit her. My mom said his face was terrible, all shriveled and twisted with rage. She had nightmares about it for a long time."

"If it had been me, I would have hit him over the head with a box of shortbreads."

"That wouldn't have been very Girl Scout–like."

"I know. But, anyway, Meat, is my mom home? I want to go back and get the binocs and these glasses that make me think. I might also take another look at Dead Oaks."

Herculeah got to her feet. She looked at Meat but he didn't move. He shook his head. "Don't go inside."

Herculeah gave him a puzzled look, sensing that he knew something she didn't.

"What's wrong? Nothing major?" She grinned.

Meat did not smile back. "I really don't think you ought to go inside."

"Oh, Meat, get out of the way."

"No." His thick fingers tightened around the banisters.

Herculeah put her hands on her hips. "Meat," she

said, "I didn't get the name Herculeah because I'm dainty and shy."

"You don't have to remind me of that."

"I got the name because I'm big and strong and I live up to my name. Now, move."

Herculeah had trained as a gymnast before she became too tall for the sport, and she still had agility, strength, and timing. She could have swung out over the railing and landed behind Meat and gone into the house. But something kept her from doing that.

"What's up?" she asked.

"There's a very suspicious-looking man in your house."

"Oh, is that all! There are always suspicious-looking people in my house. My mom's a private investigator."

"This one is different."

"How?"

"I can't explain it."

"Then get out of my way."

"This man is different," Meat said, choosing his words carefully, "because the minute I saw him I got a really bad feeling. He was like something that just—I don't know—that just crawled out from under a rock. I saw him coming down the street and I thought, Where would a creep like that be going? Then he got to your house and he stopped."

Meat stopped too, and squinted up at her. For a

moment Herculeah was startled by the look of real concern in Meat's eyes.

"Go on," she said.

"Well, the man stopped, and then he looked up and down the street before he went up your steps, as if he didn't want to be seen."

"All my mom's clients do that."

"Not like this. I've seen your mom's other clients. And when he got to the top of the steps, he turned and looked right at my house—like he knew I was watching."

"He probably did. Meat, you stand right in the window."

"I was behind the curtain this time."

"The curtain's sheer."

"I was behind the drapes! Anyway, I'm not going to tell you if you're going to pick at every word I say. I'm trying to look out for you. You sure don't know how to look out for yourself."

"I do too."

"At the mall that day—when you were on a stakeout for your mom?"

"Yes."

"Well, I was there the whole time, watching out for you."

"I saw you."

"You did not."

"You were in Wicks and Sticks."

Meat's face burned with the shame of being caught looking at candles. There was a pause, and then Herculeah said, "Get back to the man you saw."

Meat continued slowly, "His eyes were burning, and I knew he could see me. It was as if his eyes could see through things like drapes. Then he knocked at your door. Your mom answered. She drew back at the sight of him. I don't think she wanted to let him in, but she did.

"I wanted to go back in my room and check . . ." He trailed off.

That morning Meat had noticed that he had a hair on his chest. At first he thought it had fallen from his head, and he tried to brush it off. But it was attached. One dark hair was growing out of his chest. Ever since, he had been checking at regular intervals to see if this hair had been joined by another.

"I was getting ready to check something but I decided to come over here and wait for you—to tell you not to go inside."

"All right, you told me. Now, Meat, get out of the way!"

Meat stared straight ahead for a moment. He sighed. Even with a hair on his chest, he felt childish and defeated. His shoulders slumped.

"Well," he said, "don't say I didn't warn you."

3

THE MAN IN BLACK

Meat got up slowly. There was a lot of Meat, and he had to use the metal rail to pull himself to his feet.

"Thanks," Herculeah said as she slipped around him.

Meat turned to watch as she ran up the steps. "You'll be sorry," he said under his breath.

Herculeah looked down at him for a moment, her gray eyes serious. Then she grinned, "You always say that."

"And you always are."

"Well, sometimes," she admitted.

Herculeah paused at the front door. She looked

down at Meat. His face was turned away from her. His hands were on his basketball-sized knees.

Then she opened the front door. "Mom!" she called. "Mom, guess what?"

"I'm in here."

"Mom, I went in that shop on Antique Row to get the binocs"—she spoke with her usual excitement as if she thought her mother were alone—"and I saw these granny glasses and I put them on . . ."

She trailed off as she came around the doorway of the living room.

Herculeah's mother used the front two rooms of the house for her work as a private investigator. The living room was the office; the dining room was the conference room.

It was not unusual for Herculeah to come home and find her mom with a client at the dining-room table or seated in front of her desk in the living room.

However, the scene Herculeah came upon in the living room was not usual. Her mother was at her desk. Her hands were stretched out in front of her, gripping a letter opener as if she intended to use it as a weapon.

The client was not seated. He stood facing the desk, his back to Herculeah.

Herculeah drew in her breath at the size of the man. Meat had not mentioned he was huge.

He was more than huge. The man was a giant. His shoulders were hunched forward, as if to make himself less noticeable. At the end of his long, apelike arms were hands in black leather gloves.

The man still wore his overcoat. His hat was pulled down low over his forehead.

Even though Herculeah couldn't see his face, she thought there was something suspicious about the way he deliberately kept it turned away.

I am allowing Meat's fears to get to me, she told herself.

"Oh, I didn't know you had a client," Herculeah said politely. She was surprised that her voice sounded normal. "I just wanted to tell you about some eyeglasses I tried on. It can wait."

"If it's important, I can take a break."

"No."

Herculeah paused. Did her mother want to, as she put it, take a break? Her mother had never suggested such a thing before. Clients came first with her mom.

The pause lengthened. It was like one of those long pauses in a play, when the audience grows uneasy, not knowing if some actor has forgotten a line. Herculeah was certainly uneasy, and her mother was obviously tense. The man was still facing away from Herculeah, so she didn't know about him.

In that awkward pause, the man turned his head toward Herculeah. It was a slow, deliberate movement that somehow seemed threatening, like something out of a western movie.

The man's hat was black. His overcoat was black. His face turned out to be gray, as if he had never been out in the daylight or—as Meat had said—as if he had just crawled out from under a rock.

And beneath the brim of that black hat, in that gray and colorless face, were eyes that seemed to burn into Herculeah's brain. She felt as if those eyes could read her very thoughts.

She drew in her breath. A shiver of revulsion passed through her and she drew her jacket tighter, overlapping the sides as if for extra warmth.

And with those eyes burning into hers, a thought came unexpectedly to Herculeah: it's the Moloch. She drew in her breath as she remembered.

Hercules vs the Moloch was the movie her mom had been watching thirteen years ago, the day she was born. In the delivery room, her mother had told the nurse: "I'm thinking about naming this baby Hercules. Hercules Jones."

"If you do," the nurse said, "he'll turn out to be real little and the kids will tease him."

"And if it's a girl, she can be Herculeah."

"I don't think there is such a name. My little boy and I watched a Hercules movie the other night, and Samson was in it too."

The doctor said, "That's a thought. You could name her Samsonya." He broke into a Russian song. "Oh, Samson-ya!"

The nurse said, "I didn't know you could sing, Dr. Woods."

"I didn't either." There was a pause while Mrs. Jones bore down. Then the doctor said, "It's a girl!"

Her mother looked at her then and said in a sort-of surprised way: "It is Herculeah! Look how big and strong she is."

When Herculeah's mom told her that story, she ended with, "And to this day, I don't know what a Moloch looks like. I never got to see the end of the movie. I just know it's something dark and dreadful."

And now, standing in her living room was—Herculeah felt this in her bones—the Moloch.

She stared into his burning eyes.

And, she thought, it would take someone with the strength of a Hercules to get rid of him—or a Herculeah.

4

THE UNSPEAKABLE MONSTROID

Herculeah spoke to the Moloch in a voice that surprised her by still being absolutely normal.

"Oh, hi."

The Moloch cleared his throat. The sound rumbled like indoor thunder, but he didn't actually speak.

His mouth was the only straight line in his creased face. The lines across it made his lips seem to be sewed together.

"Okay, Herculeah, I'll talk to you later."

"Right."

Beyond, in the living-room window, Herculeah saw Meat's face rise like a huge worried sun. The Moloch turned his burning eyes in that direction, and Meat's round face—more worried than ever—sank.

As the Moloch saw Meat's face, he slid one gloved hand into his overcoat, the way Herculeah had seen men do on TV shows when reaching for a gun.

"It's just my friend," she said quickly. "I better go out and see what he wants."

The Moloch turned back to her and spoke. And as he spoke, his lips pulled back into a terrible grimace. His words came through his teeth, like a ventrilo-quist's.

"Your friend shouldn't be looking in other people's windows. He could get—" He paused, and the grimace grew more terrible as he finished, "let us say, arrested for things like that."

Herculeah could smell his breath and she stepped back. It wasn't bad breath—the kind that can be changed by a couple of breath mints. This was two-million-year-old breath. It was as if the air had been inhaled by a Moloch two million years ago and had now been released.

She backed further toward the hall. "I'll tell him." Then she looked at her mother. "Mom—"

"While you're at it," the Moloch interrupted, speaking through his teeth again, "tell him not to spy out his window."

"Mom—"

"Some people take," he paused as if to give emphasis to the word, "let us say, offense at being spied on. They don't like to be offended. It makes them, let us say—"

Herculeah's mother interrupted. "What were you trying to tell me, Herculeah?"

"Just that I'll be right outside, on the steps, if you need me."

Herculeah gave the Moloch an I'm-not-afraid-of-you look, turned, and started for the hall. She could feel the Moloch's eyes on her even after she had turned the corner and was out of sight. Maybe those burning eyes could see through things like drapes and walls.

She went out the front door quickly and then sank down on the top step.

Meat stuck his head around the corner of the house. "Herculeah!"

She turned in his direction.

"What did you find out?"

"Nothing."

"You had to have found out something. You were in there forever."

"All I know is what you told me. He does look creepy, and he does have burning eyes and his breath smells like"—she gave a shudder—"like million-year-old air. But you didn't tell me he was a giant!"

"I thought I did. Anyway, come over here." Meat beckoned.

"What for?"

"I can hear some of what they're saying. I think I actually heard the word . . ." He trailed off as if reluctant to say the word.

"Meat, I don't have to eavesdrop on my mom. My mom will tell me what they said. My mom is very open about things. She's actually taken me with her on stakeouts."

She brushed off her jeans. "Anyway, Meat, I saw your face in the window and so did he."

"I saw him see me."

"Yeah, but you didn't see him reach under his coat like this"—she slid her hand across her stomach—"as if he were reaching for a gun."

Meat gasped.

"Plus he said, 'Your friend shouldn't be looking in other people's windows. He could get, let us say, arrested for things like that.'"

Meat drew in his breath.

"Plus he said, 'While you're at it, tell him not to spy out his window.'"

Meat drew in another ragged breath. He did not want to hear any more pluses, but he had to ask, "He saw me then, too? I wasn't sure. I didn't want him to see me."

"Yes, and you didn't let me finish. It gets worse. He said, 'Some people take offense at being spied on. They don't like to be offended. It makes them, let us say—'"

"Let us say what?"

"I don't know. My mom interrupted him. But the Moloch is—"

Meat said quickly, "What is his name?"

"Moloch. It's not his name. It's what he is."

"What is a Moloch? I've never heard of such a thing."

"I don't know exactly. I tried to find the word once in the dictionary, but it wasn't there. I think it's a creature, some sort of unspeakable monstroid, maybe from olden times. It was in a Hercules movie."

"Unspeakable monstroid describes him all right." Meat nodded his head at Herculeah's house. "I wish he hadn't seen me."

"I do too, Meat."

"He's the kind of person that you don't even want to know you exist."

"I agree," said Herculeah.

"If you want to keep on existing."

"I didn't want to tell you this," Meat said as he sat down beside Herculeah on the steps.

"What?"

"Remember I said that I could hear some of what they were saying?"

"Yes. What did you hear?"

"I think I heard 'murder.'"

"Murder! My mother does not investigate murder! The police do that. Be real."

"Maybe this wasn't a modern murder—maybe it was something that happened in the past. All I know is the word 'murder' was mentioned."

Meat paused. In the silence that followed, he said, "What if we went in the back door very quietly and stood by the kitchen door—"

"Forget it."

"In my house, you can hear things through the heat vents. That's how I found out my mom was not taking me to see *Terminator 2*, but to the dentist. If we could find the right heat duct . . ."

"No." Herculeah sighed. "This should have been a really happy day for me. I was getting the binocs and the eyeglasses that really make me think better, but for some reason I can't enjoy it. I have an uneasy feeling."

"Me too. The Moloch knows me."

"It's not just because of the Moloch. While I was standing in front of Dead Oaks, my hair began to frizzle, and that always means I'm in danger. Only I don't know why. And when I don't know the reason for something, I'm drawn to it. I have to know." She leaned forward. "I wish I could get inside that gate."

"I know how to get in," Meat said.

Herculeah turned to him. "How?"

"Well, one time—this was Halloween—some of us wanted to toilet paper those dead trees, and I said, 'There's no way to get in,' and Howie said, 'Follow me,' and we went around back—I didn't want to go because even in the daytime that house gives me the creeps, and here it was night. But I followed along

23

with the rest of them. There were four of us, me and—" Meat broke off. "I hear him. He's coming! He's coming!" he said. "Let's hide."

"Don't be silly. I'm not hiding. This is my house."

"Well, I don't want him to see me."

Meat got up quickly and ran to the side of the house. He paused to say, "If he asks, say you haven't seen me." And he disappeared from sight.

Herculeah heard the door open behind her. She took a deep breath and got to her feet.

The Moloch came out the door, pulling his hat lower on his forehead. Herculeah stepped back against the railing to make room for him to pass. She deliberately kept her eyes on him.

She waited, expecting him to say something, dreading the smell of his two-million-year-old breath, but he went by as if she didn't exist.

At the bottom of the steps, he glanced both ways and then started toward Antique Row. Meat's face appeared around the corner of the house. The Moloch paused and looked directly at Meat.

Meat gasped. Then he said quickly, "I'm looking for my dog. You haven't seen a dog, have you?"

The Moloch didn't answer.

"It's brown with a little white spot right there." Meat touched his forehead with fingers that trembled.

"Well, thanks for your time," Meat said. "Sorry to

have bothered you." He disappeared back behind the house.

Herculeah hesitated a moment and then she ran up the steps and into the house.

Her mother was still sitting at her desk. The letter opener was clenched in her hand.

The cat, Bosco, came into the living room and jumped up on the sofa. The cat was usually curious about clients, but apparently Bosco had not liked the Moloch any more than Herculeah and Meat did.

"I can still smell him," Herculeah said, drawing in a breath. "Ugh! What a gross man."

"He's not that terrible."

"Huh! You know who I thought about when I saw him?"

"Who?"

"The Moloch!"

"Who?" Her mother looked blank, as if she had been expecting another answer.

"The Moloch. The Moloch! Don't tell me you've forgotten. You know that awful creature that Hercules had to fight?"

Her mother's shoulders seemed to relax. She smiled. "Oh, that Moloch."

"Yes. *Hercules vs the Moloch*. It was because of that movie that I got my name. How could you forget?"

"I have a lot on my mind right now, Herculeah."

"Well, so do I."

Herculeah sat down on the sofa and took Bosco on her lap. "Mom, as soon as that man turned around and looked at me, I thought, He's the Moloch, because he had this unspeakable monstroid look—well, you saw it. I don't have to describe it to you." She leaned forward eagerly. "So?"

"So what?" her mother asked.

"So what did he want?"

"It doesn't concern you, Herculeah."

Herculeah couldn't believe her ears. "What?"

"It doesn't concern you."

"Of course it concerns me. The man was in my house. He made threats against my friend—"

"The less you know about this, the better."

"Mom! Meat wanted to come in and listen through the heat vents. I said, 'No.' I said that you were very open with me. I said that was one of the best things about you. I said I didn't have to eavesdrop like other kids because you would tell me anything I wanted to know."

Her mother smiled a tired smile. "Well," she said with a shrug, "this time you were wrong."

"You're not going to tell me?"

"That's right."

"But, Mom, maybe I could help you."

"That's exactly what I'm afraid of."

"Mom, I really helped on your last case. I was the stakeout at the mall. If I had not been at the mall, you would never have located the Ryans' daughter. And—"

"This is a different kind of thing. I don't want you involved."

"I do not believe this. You know what you're teaching me to do, don't you? Eavesdrop."

Mrs. Jones braced herself on the desk and stood. She glanced down and brushed some lint from her black pantsuit.

"You and Dad are teaching me to be a sneak. First he won't tell me what's going on at Dead Oaks and now you—"

"What about Dead Oaks?"

"Dad was there this afternoon."

"What was he doing?"

"How would I know? Nobody tells me anything."

Herculeah's mother started into the hall. The cat, alerted by the activity, jumped down from Herculeah's lap. Herculeah got up and followed her mother. She changed her tactics. "Well, can I ask you one question?"

"You can ask."

"When you file this case in your filing cabinet, will you file it under M—for murder?"

6
HUSH MONEY

Herculeah watched in silence as her mother shrugged into her coat and picked up her briefcase. Her mother didn't answer.

"And is it also a big secret where you're going?"

"I'm going to the police station. I need to check on something."

"What?"

"Oh, here. Here's some money, Herculeah. What were you going to get? Oh, binoculars. And didn't you say something about eyeglasses?"

She reached into her purse and brought out her wallet. She handed Herculeah a ten-dollar bill. Then, after a moment's thought, she added another ten.

"This is bribery," Herculeah said, eyeing the money. "You're just doing this to get rid of me."

"I'm doing this because I want you to have the binoculars and whatever else you mentioned."

Herculeah didn't take the money, and her mother, smiling a little, reached out and tucked the bills into the pocket of Herculeah's jeans.

Her mother went out the door, and Herculeah followed her onto the sidewalk. Meat came around the side of the house with his hand over his heart.

"He saw me," he told Herculeah. Then to her mother, "Mrs. Jones, that guy saw me."

"I wouldn't worry about him," Herculeah's mom said as she unlocked the car. "He's got more important things on his mind."

"I said that I was looking for my dog, but I don't think he believed me."

Her mother turned. "Get your own supper, Herculeah. I might be late."

She drove off, and Herculeah and Meat stood watching the car until it disappeared.

"Who is he? Did you find out?"

"She wouldn't tell me. She gave me this." Herculeah pulled out the twenty dollars. "It was like hush money—money to shut me up."

Meat regarded the money. "So, what are you going to do?"

"I guess I'll go get the stupid binoculars and glasses," she said.

"I thought you wanted them?"

"I did. Oh, I guess I do. But it bugs me when my mom won't tell me things, because if she won't tell me, then it's something I really want to know."

"I'll walk to the store with you if that's all right," Meat said. "I don't want to be alone just now."

"Come on."

"If we see the Moloch, though, I'm splitting."

Herculeah and Meat walked side by side toward Antique Row. Herculeah was silent, bent forward, her hands stuffed in her pockets. Meat was the one to speak first.

"I get the feeling I've seen that man before."

"The Moloch?"

"Yes."

"You would have remembered."

"If I'd seen him in person, yes. But maybe I saw him on a television show."

"*Animal Kingdom*?" Herculeah asked.

Meat smiled. "Actually I was thinking of *Most Wanted*—you know, where they show pictures of criminals. If all I saw was his face, I might not have been so—well, horrified."

"Here. This is the shop." She turned in and Meat followed.

"I'm back," she said to the clerk.

"Well, that was quick. I haven't even had time to put your glasses and binoculars away. They're right here."

"Can I borrow the binoculars?" Meat asked Herculeah.

"Sure."

As Herculeah paid the clerk, Meat moved to the front of the store. He lifted the binoculars to his face. He adjusted the lenses until Dead Oaks came into focus. He felt a shiver of dread.

"See anything?"

"I don't know." Meat refocused the binoculars. "There was something in the upstairs window, but it's gone now."

"What? A face? A . . ." She couldn't think of anything else. "A what?"

"I don't know. More like a shadow. Maybe I imagined it. Anyway, it's gone now."

Herculeah and Meat went outside the store and stood for a moment under the awning.

"I think it's time for me to try my glasses. I don't know whether I told you or not, but these glasses help me think."

"Think?"

"Yes, I put on these glasses and the world becomes a blur and I think better. I fog out. It's like being in a think cocoon. I feel like I could write masterpieces and paint pictures—"

"You'd have to be able to see to paint pictures, I believe."

"Well, I would conceive of them." She took out the glasses and put them on, hooking the wires behind each ear. She was still for a moment.

"Meat!" she said.

"What? What? Where?" Meat said. He thought the Moloch was upon them. He would have dropped the binoculars if the strap hadn't been around his neck.

"They worked."

"What?"

"The eyeglasses."

"What?"

"I put them on," Herculeah said patiently, "and they made me think. They made me remember that you said you know how to get in the house."

Meat stepped backward as if alarmed by her intensity. "I didn't say house. I said gate. I said I knew how to get in the yard, but I don't want to go back in there."

"You don't have to. You just have to show me. My dad locked the gate behind him."

Meat shook his head. "I don't think I ought to."

"Well, I'll find it myself. It'll just take me longer. Give me the binoculars and go on home if you're going to be like that."

She tried to take the binoculars, and Meat was pulled forward by the strap that was still around his neck. "Give me the binoculars."

"There."

Herculeah made an elaborate display of putting the strap around her own neck. "You make such a big thing out of helping people. And now, you won't even show me how to get in a simple yard."

They glanced across the street where Dead Oaks seemed to glare back in the lengthening shadows.

"That is not a simple yard." He hesitated. Herculeah was taking a long time getting the binoculars around her neck. He said, "Anyway, how would going in that yard help people?"

"My dad said people had seen someone sneaking around the house. Maybe it was a burglar. Or a kidnapper. You were the one who saw a face in the window."

"I didn't say face!"

"Well, what else could it have been."

"Shouldn't we get the police then?"

"And look like fools if there's nobody there?"

Meat paused to choose his words. "I'd rather look like a fool than look . . . dead."

"Don't be silly."

"I never have liked deserted houses. When I'm watching TV and a person goes in an old, vacant house, I have to turn the sound off. Any little sound means there's someone in there with you." Involuntarily he shivered.

"I'm not asking you to go in the house. I'm just asking you to walk across the street and show me how to get in the yard."

Meat hesitated.

"Meat, if you're scared, then just say so."

Again Meat hesitated.

"What if there's a child in there?"

"There's not."

"There could be. And, Meat, you know how I am about children. When I'm grown I'm going to be a lawyer, and my clients are going to be children—any child that needs me." She looked at Meat. "If you were a child, held prisoner in that old house, wouldn't you want us to come get you?"

"No, I'd want the police to come get me," he said stubbornly. He squinted at her. "We could call your dad, and get him to come back."

"No. My dad—I'm sure I told you this—disapproves of my mom's work. That's one of the reasons they're divorced. My dad thinks that private investigators should mind their own business and leave the law enforcement to the police. He would just belittle me, say I'm playing detective. I hate it when he says that. 'Quit playing detective.' This is not playing."

"No," Meat agreed.

"Look," Herculeah said, "do you want to go or not?"

"I definitely do not want to go. It's one of the last things in the world I want to do." He gave a deep sigh of regret. "But, as usual, I will."

"You won't regret it," Herculeah said.

"I already do."

7
BEHIND DEAD OAKS

At dusk, Dead Oaks was even more threatening. The lengthening shadows seemed to shroud it in gloom. The dead limbs of the trees began to crackle in the breeze.

Herculeah and Meat crossed the street slowly. Meat did not dare look at the house, because his heart had started to pound in his chest the way it had two Halloweens ago.

He had not told Herculeah how terrible that night had been.

And Howie Turner had made things worse. "They say he's still in there," he had said in the low, ghost-story voice he used to terrify boys at Camp Okee-chobie around the campfire.

"He can't be. He's dead," Richie had answered. "Isn't he?"

"Nobody saw him leave."

"He's dead. My dad said."

"Then if he's dead and he didn't leave—he's still in there—somewhere—waiting!" This was said in the same spine-chilling voice. Meat had thought Howie Turner could be the host of *Chiller Theater*.

In the dark Meat had bumped into Richie, causing Richie to scream in fright.

"Cut it out, will you?" Howie said. "What do you think this is—Halloween?" Even though it was Halloween, no one said a word of rebuttal.

When he had recovered somewhat, Richie went on in a slightly higher voice, "My daddy told me that one time they got the police to go through the house."

"And you know what they found, don't you?" Howie interrupted.

The boys waited, their Halloween disguises making them feel more vulnerable than frightening.

"They found that his clothes were in the closet. They found that his food was on the table. They found that his money was in his wallet. They found that his books were on the shelf. They found everything but one thing."

They waited, breathless.

"Him!"

The details had made Meat shiver two years ago, and they had the same effect on him now. He tried to zip up his jacket and found it was already zipped.

Meat cleared his throat as he led Herculeah down the alley to the back of the house. He felt there was something in his throat that didn't want to go down.

"They say that they don't know what happened to him," Meat said.

"Right," Herculeah answered. "He just disappeared. They wanted to sell the house or do something with it, my mom said, only they found they couldn't. I don't know the exact details."

Again Meat attempted to swallow. He paused at the old gate where he and his friends had slipped through two years ago.

Back then, Meat had been hopeful that because of his size he wouldn't be able to slip through, but the efforts of all the boys had finally moved the back gate, and he had to go inside.

"This is it?" Herculeah said.

"Right. I might not be able to squeeze through because—you know—because of my size. I could hardly squeeze through two years ago, and I was smaller then."

Herculeah reached out and pulled the gate open

easily. He should have known she would have the strength of at least three boys.

"No problem," she said.

They paused. The only sound was Meat zipping his jacket up and down.

"Houses like this give me the creeps," he said.

"Well, I don't exactly love them."

"Yes, you do. You know there's not a child in there. You know there is not one reason for you to go in except that you want to."

Herculeah shrugged.

They looked up at the house together. The windows were dark, the sandstone walls black with age.

"Oh, I wish I'd brought my mom's keys," Herculeah said.

"What?"

"My mom has keys that can get her in anywhere."

"You said you just wanted to go in the yard. You didn't say anything about going inside."

"I'm talking about the next time we come. I'll bring them next time. Come on."

Herculeah slipped through the gate and into the overgrown yard. Meat hesitated, as he had two years ago.

Despite the years, he again heard Howie's cruel words ring through the deserted yard. "Blubber's scared."

"I am not!" he cried.

Herculeah turned to look at him. "You are not what?"

"Oh, nothing."

He followed her across the yard, picking his way through the overgrowth and garbage.

"Nobody's been through here in years."

"That's the way it looks," Herculeah admitted.

"So there couldn't be anybody inside. We ought to go. We shouldn't be doing this. We—"

Herculeah ran forward. "Oh, look, Meat, here's the cellar door—and it's wood. It's rotten around the hinges. I bet if we pulled . . ."

"No."

"Meat, come on. Help me!"

"No! This is breaking and entering! This is a criminal act."

"Then stand back."

Meat retreated a few steps. His three friends had worked on this old door for a long time and had gotten nowhere, so perhaps Herculeah wouldn't have any success either.

She managed to open it on her second try. "There," she said.

Slowly she pulled open the door. It creaked, and behind her Meat shuddered at the sound. The smell of musty air came from the inside.

Meat stepped back. "I don't feel good. Just the smell of an old house like this . . . I'm very sensitive to smells. If they ever put smells on TV, I won't be able to watch anymore. Like on the Discovery Channel when they're showing bears eating fish? The smell would make me faint. Unless, of course, there would be some way to turn the smell down the way you can turn the sound down. Or, say, someone was in the dentist's chair and you know how scary dentists' offices smell, well, I wouldn't—"

"Meat, stop babbling."

"I'm sorry. I can't help it."

Herculeah peered at him through the dusk. "You do look sort of pale."

Meat nodded.

"All right, you better stay out here."

"You mean I don't have to go in?" He sagged with relief. "I can go home?"

"No, you can't go home. You have to stand out here and be the lookout."

"Oh."

"Let's see." Herculeah glanced around the backyard.

"Stand over there on the other side of the fence by the back of the hardware store, and if you see anybody, give me a signal."

"I'll give one of my whistles." Meat was proud of his whistles. They could be heard blocks away. It was the only thing he could do better than Herculeah.

"No, that's too obvious. I know, knock one of those garbage cans over—and really knock it over, Meat, because I might not hear it inside. Make a lot of racket."

"I will. You'll hear it."

Herculeah watched Meat slip through the gate, cross the alley, and stand like a sentry beside the garbage cans. She signaled him to get down lower, out of sight.

Slowly Meat sank down in the shadows and leaned his head back against the hardware store. The relief of not having to go inside Dead Oaks made him suddenly drowsy.

If he didn't have to be on the lookout for Herculeah, he thought he might even fall asleep.

Herculeah gave him a wave. He peered around the garbage can to watch.

Herculeah turned to the basement doorway. She stared into the dim interior and there was something about the way she stood . . . It was as if she were going into a place of entertainment.

Meat saw her take a deep breath. The thought of the terrible air she was breathing made Meat lean back against the store. This time his eyes closed.

At the cellar door of Dead Oaks, Herculeah squared her shoulders. She slipped inside and disappeared into the gloom.

8

SOMEONE AT THE GATE

Herculeah paused just inside the basement door, and the dark room seemed to close in around her. She waited for her eyes to adjust to the darkness. She wished for a flashlight. The next time she came, she would bring one.

She started a mental list:

Keys

Flashlight

From the glow of the street lights by the hardware store she could see that she was in a sort of workshop area. But it was an artificial light that gave the room an eery, misty look.

Around her were old gardening tools: a wheel-barrow, rakes and shovels, an old hand lawn mower. There was a worktable to the right.

Herculeah was not interested in the contents of the basement. What she wanted to find was an entrance into the upstairs of the house. She knew the door to the upstairs would be locked, but that was what keys were for. She could come back with her mother's keys.

From the moment she had stood in front of Dead Oaks and felt her hair rise, she had been drawn here. It wasn't just that an old man's body had never been found. She had been aware of that for years. But the events of today had somehow made her a part of the mystery. There was something about this house that she had to know.

"You never give up," her mother had said to her once, and she had answered, "Well, I got that from you and Dad." Both statements were true.

I have to know, she said silently. I can't stand not to know things. A man doesn't just disappear. There has to be a reason.

Herculeah heard a sound in the corner. She paused.

Something small scurried out of the way, deeper into the debris. Herculeah hesitated. She was not afraid of mice, and yet she listened for a moment. Had there been another noise . . . outside?

She shook her head. Her mind was playing tricks. At

least, she hadn't heard a garbage can being overturned.

She continued deeper into the basement.

Outside, by the hardware store, Meat's eyes were so heavy he couldn't hold them open.

He sighed. His eyes closed in sleep just as the dark figure of a man came out of the shadows and stopped at the gate of Dead Oaks.

9
FOOTSTEPS

In the basement Herculeah moved past a stone deer that had once, she imagined, graced the lawn. She rested one hand on the fawn's head. Again she paused to listen. She heard nothing.

Slowly working a path around the tools and boxes, she made her way to the end of the room and stopped at the wall. She lifted her hands and laid them flat against the cool concrete.

She moved sideways, feeling for an opening. The cellar was darkest here. Her fingers felt cobwebs, and she brushed her hands together. Herculeah wasn't afraid of spiders either.

She moved the length of the wall, but she found no door. This was just one room—a toolshed, a work area—separate from the rest of the house.

Disappointed, Herculeah turned. The doorway was lit from the hardware store, but the rest of the basement was completely dark now. There was nothing more to do here. She started forward.

At that moment she heard footsteps outside. The footsteps were coming toward the house.

Fear stabbed at her.

Herculeah ducked quickly behind the stone deer. She held her breath. Her heart began to pound.

She knew her hair must be going wild, and this was not the time for it. She drew her expanding hair against her head like a cap.

For a brief moment, she thought it might be Meat. She hoped it was Meat. She desperately longed to see his round silhouette in the doorway, to hear him say, "Herculeah, aren't you finished yet? I'm tired of waiting. I want to go home."

She wanted to call Meat's name, but something about the heaviness of the steps held her back. Meat was large but he walked lightly. It was not Meat who was coming toward her with those slow, threatening steps.

She waited. She thought about that old ghost story that had scared her as a child: "I'm on the first step. . . .

I'm on the second step. . . . I'm on the third step. . . ."

But if it wasn't Meat, she wondered, why hadn't Meat sounded the alarm? Why hadn't he knocked over the garbage can to warn her?

She wanted to lift her head, but she didn't dare. Even with her head pressed against her knees, with her eyelids squeezed shut, she knew the exact moment the person got to the basement door.

The door had been left open, but it creaked as if someone bigger than Herculeah was planning to come in. There was a terrible silence as the person stood, looking inside.

Herculeah's heart had moved up into her throat.

Nothing happened. The awful moment stretched on and on. Silently Herculeah glanced around the side of the deer.

Silhouetted in the doorway was a man. Highlighted by the strange misty light, the man looked huge. Herculeah drew in her breath. He was more than huge. He was a giant.

He ducked his head to peer into the basement.

Herculeah rested her forehead against the cold stone of the deer. There had been something frightening and familiar about that shape.

The man reached into his pocket and brought out a cigarette lighter. There was a faint click, and in the glow from the small flame, Herculeah saw his face. It was the Moloch.

Her knees began to tremble. She had to breathe through her mouth to get enough air.

The Moloch came into the basement and stopped. Herculeah cringed as he lifted the lighter and its pale glow touched the objects around her. She clutched her hair tighter about her head.

The Moloch did not come back to where she crouched in fear. Instead he moved over to the workbench. He stood there, and then, as if he were familiar with the table, he picked up something, opened a drawer, and took something from it. Herculeah longed to stand up so she could see, but she remembered the burning look of the Moloch's eyes in her living room, the fear she had felt at his terrible smile. She stayed where she was.

Her heart was beating so loud, it pounded in her ears.

Apparently, the Moloch had found what he needed. Herculeah heard him move toward the door. She heard him take a step outside.

Herculeah lifted her head. Silhouetted against the light from the parking lot, she saw him raise his arm. For one terrible moment, Herculeah thought he had seen her and was lifting his arm in a terrible and final gesture of farewell.

But the moment lengthened. He seemed to be reaching for something. She heard a faint crumbling sound. What was he doing? Why didn't he leave?

She didn't move. The Moloch lowered his arm, and Herculeah heard the faint click as he extinguished the cigarette lighter. She heard the creaking sound as the Moloch began to close the door.

Herculeah had a moment of such relief that she felt weak. The Moloch hadn't seen her. The Moloch was leaving. And just as soon as he was gone, she could leave too. She could get Meat and—

Then Herculeah froze.

For she heard something that turned her blood cold. She heard the sound of hammering.

The Moloch was nailing the door shut.

And she was trapped inside.

10

THE MAN WHO WAS NOT A DREAM

Meat awoke, and for a moment he didn't know where he was. His body felt stiff and uncomfortable, the way it did when he fell asleep on the floor watching TV. He hated that, especially when the channel had gone off the air and he was faced with a screen of snow.

But this was worse. There was no screen, and the world itself seemed to have lost its color. Everything was sort of white.

Meat tried not to panic. Perhaps something had gone wrong with his eyes. He rubbed them, but there was no change.

"What is this?" he murmured.

All the good colors in the world—the ones he found so restful—the blues and greens—had faded, and he was left in a world of grayish-white.

It was like the time the color on the TV set had gone bad, and for weeks—until his mother got the money for repair—he had watched a world of gray. All his favorites, even Norm on *Cheers,* had been pale and insignificant.

Well, he knew one thing. Wherever he was, he had to get out of there. He had to get home.

He rolled over, bracing himself on one knee, and staggered to his feet. He stumbled clumsily.

As he struggled for balance, he knocked over something, something big. It felt like a—maybe a garbage can.

The sound was an explosion in the quiet night. The metal crashed against the pavement. Then the lid fell off and clattered around and around.

Meat put his hands to his ears. What was this terrible noise? Where was he?

At that moment he came fully awake. He remembered it all. He was here on sentry duty. He closed his eyes in dismay as the full horror of the situation washed over him.

Herculeah had gone into the basement of Dead Oaks. And his part in the disaster was to stand watch and turn over the garbage can if anyone came. She had trusted him. And he, like a fool, had fallen asleep and knocked over the garbage can by accident.

Herculeah would be furious with him. He began to create a quick story.

"I thought I saw someone. I swear I thought I saw someone. Maybe it was a shadow. Oh, all right, it was a shadow but it was right at the gate. I thought it was a big man. Or maybe I dreamed it. I have to admit I did doze off for a second—"

He opened his eyes. He began to feel a little better.

"That's it. I thought I saw someone at the gate, and I didn't want to take any chances and so I knocked the garbage can over. Your life is very valuable to me, Herculeah."

His eyes began to focus and he looked down the alley. He expected to see Herculeah running toward him.

Instead, he found, to his dismay, that the story he had created was true. There was someone at the gate. It was a big man, a very big man.

Meat paused, frozen with fear. The man turned in the direction of the parking lot. The lid of the garbage can was still clattering at Meat's feet, drawing attention to his unfortunate position.

Meat wanted to duck down, but there was nothing big enough for him to duck behind. He froze. He knew how animals felt caught in the headlights of a car, waiting to be clobbered.

The man was bound to be able to see him. He was in the light.

But Meat couldn't see the man clearly. He was in the shadows. All he could see was that the man was large and he had on dark clothes.

Maybe, Meat thought, the man was some sort of night watchman—they wore dark clothes—or a policeman. He would have to think up a pretty good story if it was a policeman.

"I was on my way home from a Boy Scout meeting, sir, and I didn't feel well and I decided to sit down for a moment and—"

Maybe it would even be Herculeah's dad. And Herculeah's dad would forbid her to do these dangerous things, and they could all go home and have hot chocolate.

The figure began to walk toward him. The steps were slow and heavy.

It was not a policeman or a night watchman or Herculeah's dad. With increasing dread, Meat made out a huge man in a black coat and a black hat.

His mouth dropped open. It was the last person in the world Meat wanted to see. It was the Moloch.

Meat stepped back. He found himself flat against the wall of the hardware store.

He had a moment of terrible decision. He didn't know whether to run or to—

He tried hard, but he couldn't think of another choice. Running was the only thing to do.

The Moloch was still coming toward him in that slow, heavy way, one step at a time.

Meat knew that in a few more steps, he would be able to see those burning, terrible eyes. He made a decision.

He pulled himself away from the hardware store, turned, ran around the corner of the store and headed for home.

At the corner he turned and ran backward a few steps to see if the Moloch was still following. He was not in sight.

"I'll be back," he called over his shoulder. He hoped Herculeah could hear him in that musty black basement.

Well, he thought, at least he had warned her. He *had* knocked over the garbage can.

His heart raced with fear and with a determination to, once again, save Herculeah.

He paused in front of the House of Cards store. He put his fingers in his mouth. He would give a whistle so loud it would shatter windows, wake the dead, cause dogs all over the county to bay at the moon.

He blew but nothing happened. For the first time in his life his whistle failed. He knew the truth. A person could get too scared to whistle.

11

HERCULEAH IN THE DARK

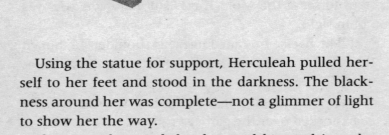

Using the statue for support, Herculeah pulled herself to her feet and stood in the darkness. The blackness around her was complete—not a glimmer of light to show her the way.

She stepped around the deer and bumped into the wheelbarrow. There was a thud as her knee hit the metal.

Herculeah froze, waiting to see if that sound would bring the Moloch back. In the seconds that followed she noticed three things.

1. There were no footsteps coming back to the house.
2. Her knee was beginning to throb where she had struck it on the wheelbarrow.

And 3. Someone, somewhere, had just turned over a garbage can.

"Now you warn me," Herculeah said. "Why didn't you warn me when I could have done something about it. Meeeeat!"

She broke off and listened to make sure neither the Moloch nor Meat was coming. Then she began to grope her way toward the door.

Her hands touched rakes and shovels. She found a hoe, a trowel.

In all these tools, she thought, there has to be a pickax or a hatchet. If she could get her hands on something sharp, she could hack at the door until it gave. The wood was half rotten.

She felt garden hoses, the old lawn mower—nothing she could use. By now she had made her way to the door.

She put her hands against the wood and rested for a moment. No sounds came from the yard. She wondered if the Moloch was gone, or if he was still outside, waiting at the gate.

If she could get the door open, she knew she could get away. The Moloch was huge, but she was fast. If she could break out of the basement, she could streak across the yard and vault over the fence. She wouldn't have to bother with the gate.

She took a deep breath. She rested one shoulder

against the door and pushed slightly, testing the strength of the wood.

There was some give in it. The nails might not hold. He had only put in one or two.

Herculeah pulled back and rammed her shoulder into the door. Pain shot up to her neck. She drew back and pushed again, again.

It took four tries, and then, with a screeching sound, the door burst open. Herculeah staggered out into the cool night air. She stood for a moment, bent forward, gasping for breath.

She looked up, ready to run, but the Moloch was nowhere in sight. She didn't take any chances. She decided to run anyway.

Herculeah streaked across the yard, the weeds whipping around her ankles. She got to the fence, grasped the metal rail, and vaulted cleanly over it.

She ran down the alley and out onto the sidewalk. She looked around wildly, but the Moloch was not in sight.

There were just ordinary people, doing ordinary things, driving cars, looking in shop windows, coming out of the frozen yogurt shop, eating cones.

Herculeah stopped her desperate run and paused to catch her breath. After a moment she began to jog for home.

As she turned the corner onto her street, she saw

Meat and his mother coming toward her. They were walking fast.

Meat's mother had a frying pan in one hand—her weapon of choice. Meat held a baseball bat that had never swatted a ball.

Herculeah called, "I'm all right." She ran to join them.

"What happened?" Meat asked, walking forward to meet her.

"He nailed the door shut. I was inside that basement with the door nailed shut. Then, *then* you knocked over the garbage can."

"I didn't see him when he went in," Meat admitted truthfully. "He nailed you in there?"

"Right."

"How did you get out?"

"I just put my shoulder to the door and pushed."

"You broke out?"

Herculeah nodded. "The door was rotten. You saw how easy it was for me to get in."

"Then what?"

"Then I started for home, and here I am."

"The Moloch wasn't there when you got out?"

She shook her head.

Meat's mother said, "I do not like having to come out with my frying pan after you kids. I want you kids to behave yourselves."

"But thank you for doing it," Herculeah said.

Meat's mother turned and walked away. Over her shoulder she said, "Albert, you come home now. Herculeah's gotten you in enough trouble for one night."

"I'm coming."

"What we've got to do next time—" Herculeah began when his mother was in the house and out of earshot, but Meat interrupted.

"Next time? Next time? Are you crazy? Have you gone absolutely mad?"

"No, I am not mad."

"Well, you look like it."

She put her hands to her hair and tried to smooth it into place. She probably did look wild. But then she had every reason to. She looked coolly at Meat.

Meat looked back. He was weak with fright and tension. This had been the most terrifying night of his life. It had been far, far worse than that terrible Halloween two years ago.

He kept looking into Herculeah's gray eyes and spoke with unusual sarcasm. "Why don't you go in the house and put on those glasses. You really do need something to make you think!"

And he went up the stairs to his house and closed the door.

12
ABOUT DEAD OAKS

Herculeah looked in the hall mirror. She smiled at herself.

She looked much better now. She had showered and washed her hair and combed it back into a ponytail.

When she had first come into the house and caught sight of her face in the hall mirror she had been startled. Meat had been right. She did look slightly mad.

Her hair stood out from her head and was coated with cobwebs. Her face was smeared with dirt. Her breathing hadn't gotten back to normal. And excitement always brought a certain wild gleam to her eyes.

She was glad that her mother hadn't been there to see her. She also hoped that Meat's mom would not come over in the morning and say, "I had to go out with my frying pan after that daughter of yours last night."

Herculeah had put on a Chinese robe she had bought at Goodwill. She didn't like to shop in the stores at the mall—The Gap and The Limited. She liked different clothes.

She took one last glance in the mirror. She was pleased with the way she looked, and she went downstairs to wait for her mother.

Herculeah was sitting on the sofa, thinking back over the evening, when she remembered Meat's last words.

"Why don't you go in the house and put on those glasses. You really do need something to make you think!" he had said.

Meat was being sarcastic, but it wasn't a bad idea. She went to the hall closet and took her eyeglasses from her jacket pocket.

As she walked back to the sofa, she fastened the slender hooks behind her ears.

She sat down and stared into the thick, pale glass circles. The world disappeared in a kind of pleasant haze, and Herculeah waited for the magic—for the thoughts to burst into her brain the way they had earlier in Hidden Treasures.

She was just beginning to feel the first stirrings of thought when she heard her mother's car out front, and the process was interrupted.

"Mom, I'm in here," she called.

Her mother appeared in the doorway. "I thought you'd be in bed."

"I wasn't sleepy. I wanted to wait up for you."

"Well, I am sleepy. Turn out the lights when you come up." She looked at Herculeah more closely. "Are those the glasses you bought today?"

"Yes."

"You can't see out of them. I know you can't. Why on earth would you spend good money to be blind?"

"You've missed the whole point, Mom."

"Obviously."

"They don't make me blind, they allow me to think. I fog out."

"Then the money was certainly well spent." Now her mother was being sarcastic.

Herculeah took off the glasses and followed her mother to the stairs. "Can I ask you something?"

"I'm tired, Herculeah."

"This is not a tiring sort of question—just something sort of historical I want to know."

"What?"

"I'm curious about Dead Oaks."

"Oh?"

"That's the old house Dad was at today."

"I'm aware of that."

"It used to be called Twin Oaks, but now everybody calls it—"

Her mother looked at Herculeah. Her tired eyes were suddenly sharp. "Why are you so interested in that house all of a sudden?"

"It's not all of a sudden," Herculeah said defensively. "I've always been curious about that house. Meat was talking about it tonight. He said that some boys told him the old man disappeared."

"I wouldn't know."

"Meat said that some boys told him that the police went in the house and didn't find anything. There was food on the table and money in his wallet, but the man wasn't there."

"It was in the newspaper. I don't remember all the details." Her mother turned and continued up the stairs.

Herculeah followed. "I remember there was some sort of legal document—you're bound to know something about that. You're into legal documents."

"Oh, all right," her mother said, relenting a little. "Let's see. There was a will, and it stated that the house could not be sold or disposed of until after his funeral. And since there has been no funeral—there couldn't be, there has been no dead body—the house remains."

"Meat said that when the police went in, he wasn't there. Do you think he could have been hiding?"

"I imagine if that old man did not want to be found, he wouldn't be found."

"Then he could still be in there."

"Theoretically. The power is still on. The water's still on."

"How do you know that?"

"I did some checking."

"Tonight?"

"How could I check tonight? Everything's closed."

"You have your ways."

Her mother gave a noncommittal shrug.

"This afternoon Dad said that people had seen someone around the house. Maybe the old man is still there."

"Oh, Herculeah, the man's probably a hundred years old—if he's still alive. Now, let's go to bed, please?"

"All right, but Mom, can I ask you just one more thing?"

"What now?"

"Did he have a family?"

"He was married, yes. His wife's dead. She did have a funeral."

"Did he have children?"

"Good night, Herculeah."

"But—"

"Good night!"

"Oh, all right. Good night, Mom," Herculeah answered.

Herculeah remained outside her mother's door for a moment until she heard the sound of the bedsprings creaking and knew her mother was in bed.

"Just one more thing. What date was it—when the police went in Dead Oaks?"

"September 1983," her mother called back.

From the way her mother answered, Herculeah knew that whatever date it was, it was not September 1983.

"Thanks."

Herculeah went into her bedroom. She sat on the window seat for a moment, looking across the street at Meat's darkened house.

"Yes, Meat, there is going to have to be a next time. And," she added, "if you won't go with me, I'll go alone."

13
OLD MAN CREWELL

"My mom almost didn't allow me to come over to your house," Meat said.

Meat and Herculeah were in the Jones's kitchen, sitting across from each other at the table. Herculeah held the phone in one hand. She was preparing to dial.

She gave him a disgusted look. "Meat, that's like in second grade when she wouldn't allow me to play with you because of my mud bomb factory."

"No, this is different," Meat said. "My mom really thinks there is something dangerous about Dead Oaks."

"She's just mad because the old man wouldn't buy any of her Girl Scout cookies."

"I'm not so sure she isn't right."

"She thought there was something dangerous about mud bombs too."

"And there was."

"Not unless I was throwing them. You had terrible aim."

Meat paused, considering whether to defend his aim or to continue with what his mother said. Finally he decided.

"She says that everybody in that family has disappeared mysteriously: the old man, the son, the wife—well, the wife died, but there was something mysterious about the way that happened as well."

"So there was a child," Herculeah said to herself. "A son."

"Yes, but there was something funny about—"

Herculeah interrupted, "Oh, be quiet, Meat. The phone's ringing."

"Zone Three Police Precinct," the voice on the other end of the line said, "Captain Morrison speaking."

"Hi, Captain Morrison, this is Herculeah Jones. Is my dad, Chico, busy?"

"I'll check, Herculeah."

To Meat, she said, "He's checking. My dad must be there or—"

"Herculeah," it was her father's voice, and she leaned forward. "What's up?"

"Oh, nothing, Dad. I just wanted to ask you a quick question."

"Shoot."

"Do you remember yesterday when I caught you over at Dead Oaks?"

"I wouldn't say you caught me there."

"Well, I was just wondering what was the name of the people who lived there."

Meat said, "The name's Crewell."

To Meat, Herculeah mouthed the words, "I know."

"Crewell," her father said. "The old man was sort of a legend in his time."

"Didn't the police go in there once? I think somebody thought he might be dead."

"I believe so."

"Did you go?"

"No."

"Oh, I wish you had. Then you could fill me in on things."

"It is not my job to fill you in on things."

"I know, but will you do me one favor?"

"What?"

"Would you check and find out when that happened?"

"And I suppose you want me to drop what I'm doing and check on it right this minute?"

"Yes."

"Actually I pulled that file up yesterday. It's here somewhere."

There was a pause while her father put down the phone, and Herculeah turned to Meat. "He's going to find out. And then we'll go—"

Meat stood up so fast his chair tipped over backward. "No," he said. "No."

"Meat . . ."

He began to back up. "No," he said again, shaking his head this time.

"Oh, Meat, sit down. We're not going back to Dead Oaks, if that's what you're thinking. Sit down!"

Meat stayed in the doorway, ready to leave for home at any minute.

"I promise we're not going to the house. We're going to—Oh, hi, Dad."

"I got it," her father said. "It was October 4, 1990."

"Any details?"

"No. It just says they obtained a court order to search the premises. This was in response to an anonymous letter."

"What did the letter say?"

"Let's see. It's right here. 'There is somebody dead in Twin Oaks. Look down the dark stairs.' That's it."

Herculeah repeated, "'There is somebody dead in Twin Oaks. Look down the dark stairs.'"

In the doorway, Meat shivered.

"Yes. Big printing, like it was written by a child."

"But you don't think it was a child?"

"No."

"So they checked and didn't find anything?"

"Yes. There was a broken window upstairs. I believe someone was going to have it repaired."

"And there was no body?"

"That's right."

"But, Dad, if there was a body—I mean, wouldn't there have been a terrible smell?"

"Depends. There was a case out in Marietta where this woman died in her kitchen. Her neighbors thought she had gone to a nursing home and they cut her grass and kept the place up. Four years later somebody went inside and found her on the kitchen floor."

"Dead?"

"Yes. The phone was in her hand. I guess she was trying to call for help. Why are you so interested in this, Herculeah?"

"It's too complicated to explain."

"I'm used to complicated things. Go ahead."

"Oh, I'll tell you about it later. Meat's here and we're going out. I've got to run now."

"How about the basketball game next weekend? You interested?"

"Yeah, Dad, I'd like that a lot. I'll talk to you later."

Herculeah hung up the phone, and looked up at

Meat. There was a look of determination in her gray eyes that he didn't like.

Meat raised both hands as if for protection. He said, "I am not going back to that house, Herculeah—ever. My mom made me promise I wouldn't and, believe me, she did not have to twist my arm. She said, 'Meat, I want you to promise me you will never go to that house.' And before she could finish, I'd promised."

"We are not going to the house."

"I don't believe you. It's a trick. You'll—"

"We're going to the public library, Meat. Is that safe enough?"

She passed him.

"Even the public library wouldn't be safe with you," he mumbled before he followed.

14

A FACE IN THE CROWD

"You read it aloud," Herculeah said. "I'm going to put on my glasses so I can think better."

She took her eyeglasses from her pocket and lifted them to her face.

"Could I try those?" Meat asked.

Herculeah looked at him. "Yes, but be careful. They're fragile."

Meat and Herculeah were in the periodical room of the library. The old newspapers were on microfilm, and Herculeah had threaded in the reel and located the article of October 5, 1990.

There was a picture of the crowd outside Dead Oaks, but on the microfilm it looked like a negative.

Meat put on the eyeglasses while Herculeah watched. He peered through the thick glasses. His face was pulled into an expression of deep concentration.

"So," Herculeah asked after a moment, "what are you thinking?"

"Nothing."

"Meat, you can't be thinking of nothing. Even when you're asleep, you're thinking of something."

"I was thinking of nausea. I'm getting sort of nauseated."

"Take my glasses off, this minute. Give them here." She spoke as if he had offended her.

"I'm sorry."

Herculeah took the glasses and hooked them behind her ears. She stared through the thick glass.

"Go ahead," she said, "read it aloud."

Meat bent closer to the screen. He cleared his throat and glanced over his shoulder to see if the noise had disturbed any of the other library patrons. Lowering his voice, he began to read.

"'A crowd gathered this morning in front of the Crewell house on Antique Row as police entered the residence. This was in response to an anonymous letter to the police.' It doesn't quote the letter, but we know what it said. 'There is somebody dead in Twin Oaks. Look down the dark stairs.'" Meat knew it by heart now.

"Read the newspaper story, Meat."

"'Hamilton Crewell, the owner of the residence, has not been seen in several years, and there was speculation that he might be ill.'"

"Or dead," Herculeah interrupted.

"Yes, I think that's why there was such a crowd. For some reason people like to see other people being carried out in body bags. Why that is, I don't know."

"Me either. Go on, Meat."

"'The police went through the entire house, but were unable to locate Mr. Crewell or any signs of foul play.'"

"No signs of foul play," Herculeah repeated. "You know what that means. No blood, no dead bodies, no weapon on the premises, no threatening note."

Meat looked at her with respect. "Those glasses do work," he said.

Herculeah said, "The police report said there was a broken window upstairs, but that was the extent of the damage. Keep reading."

"There's just one more paragraph. 'Hamilton Crewell, a retired businessman, has been a recluse since the unfortunate accident resulting in the death of his wife, Edna Foster Crewell.'"

"I wonder what the unfortunate accident was."

"It doesn't say."

"That's it?"

"Yes."

Herculeah sat without moving, staring intently into her thick glasses.

"Are you still thinking?" Meat asked, finally breaking the silence.

"I'm trying to."

"You want me to be quiet?"

"It would help. What I want to find out," she went on slowly, "is about the death of his wife. Lots of times things are connected. My mom told me that. My dad too. Always look for the connection."

Meat turned back to the screen. He looked at the picture of the crowd in front of the house. He scanned the faces.

Suddenly he gasped and drew back.

Herculeah whipped off her glasses and looked at him. "What is it now?"

"Look."

Herculeah sighed. "What is it I'm supposed to be looking at?"

"The picture."

She bent forward. "Oh, that. I saw it. It's just a crowd of people."

"I think you better look again. I didn't see this at first, because it's like a negative, but we know somebody in that crowd of people."

Herculeah began to search the faces.

"Someone we wish we didn't know."

"In the front or back?"

"I'll give you a hint," Meat said. "The one we know has got on a black hat and it's pulled down low on his face, like he doesn't want to be recognized, but he's so big nobody could miss him."

Herculeah drew in a ragged breath.

At the back of the crowd, standing alone, towering over the others, was a man with a black hat pulled down low on his face.

"The Moloch," she said.

"Yes, the Moloch! That man keeps turning up in my life. I want to get away from him, but I can't. Even in the public library."

"It's just a picture."

They bent forward to look again.

"What do you think he was doing there?" Meat asked.

"The same thing as the other people—waiting to see if old man Crewell was brought out in a body bag."

"But why?"

"I don't know," Herculeah said, "but when I was in that basement and the Moloch came in, it was like he was familiar with the place. He went right over to the workbench and got the hammer and nails. I think he had been there before."

"But what's the connection?"

"That's what we've got to find out."

15
TAPED

Herculeah had been sitting on the sofa with her glasses on since they got back from the library, staring into the thick circles of glass. So far she had not had one single thought.

"At least I'm not getting nauseated," she said to herself.

Herculeah had wanted to talk to her mom, but her mom had already left the house. So Herculeah had not been able to get any answers from her. She had to depend on these glasses to make her think.

"Think," she told her brain.

The phone rang. Herculeah slipped her glasses up

on her head and moved to her mother's desk to answer it.

"Mim Jones's office," she said.

There was no response.

"Mim Jones's office."

Again there was no answer. Then a low, hesitant voice said, "Is she there?"

Herculeah would have recognized that voice anywhere. The Moloch. Her heart began to pound as it had the night before in the basement of Dead Oaks.

She said, "She can't take your call right now," as her mother had instructed her to do. Her mother's advice, "Never let anyone know you're here alone," seemed to fit the occasion.

"When will she be back?" the Moloch said.

"I'm expecting her at any moment."

Again there was a pause.

"Can I take a message?" Herculeah asked.

"Yes."

"What?"

"The key is still there."

She heard a click on the other end of the line and then the dial tone.

She hung up the phone, sat, and leaned back in her mother's swivel chair. She drew her glasses back onto her face.

And at that moment, the glasses worked. A thought made Herculeah sit up abruptly.

She remembered her mother's tape recorder. Why hadn't she thought of that before? Her mother had a tape recorder under her desk, and she often taped her conversations with clients—sometimes with their permission, sometimes without.

Perhaps she had taped her conversation yesterday with the Moloch.

Reaching under the desk, Herculeah felt the tape recorder and punched the Rewind button. Then she punched Play.

Her mother's voice came from the tape. "I charge thirty dollars an hour, plus expenses."

"What expenses? You just need to get inside the house and find the body."

"It may be that simple, but the police came up empty-handed."

"That's why I'm here."

"And I require an advance of—"

Herculeah clicked off the tape. This was the end of the conversation. She rewound the tape.

The Moloch was speaking.

"Your friend shouldn't be looking in other people's windows. He could get—let us say, arrested for things like that."

Then her own voice. "I'll tell him. Mom—"

"While you're at it, tell him not to spy out his window."

"Mom—"

"Some people take—let us say, offense at being spied on. They don't like to be offended. It makes them, let us say—"

Herculeah stopped the tape. This was the conversation that had taken place while she was in the room. She wasn't interested in that. She rewound the tape to the beginning. This time she got what she wanted.

Her mother's voice said, "What can I do for you, Mr. . . . ?" Her mother paused, giving the man time to supply his name.

"Smith."

Herculeah knew, from the brief pause before he spoke, that the man's name was not Smith.

"How can I help you, Mr. Smith?"

"I want you to find something for me."

"What?"

"A body."

"Whose body is that?"

The man hesitated. And while Herculeah waited for the answer, the phone rang.

With a sigh of impatience, Herculeah pushed Pause on the recorder and picked up the phone. She hoped it wasn't the Moloch again.

"Mim Jones's office."

Meat's voice said, "You want to come over and watch TV? *Oprah*'s got private investigators on, and one of them is investigating—"

"I don't care what they're investigating, Meat. Guess what I'm doing?"

"What?"

"I am listening to the conversation between my mom and the Moloch."

"Your mom taped that conversation?"

"Yes."

"Yesterday's conversation?"

"Yes."

"The one she wouldn't tell you about?"

"Yes!"

"I'll be right over," Meat said.

16

THE MISSING BODY

"Start the tape from the beginning," Meat said. He made himself as comfortable as possible on the footstool beside Herculeah's chair.

There was a whir as Herculeah reached under the desk and rewound the tape. She punched the Play button, and her mother's voice came from the recorder.

"What can I do for you, Mr. . . .?"

"Smith."

Meat said, "I bet that's not his real name."

Herculeah put one finger to her lips to silence him. The recorder continued.

"How can I help you, Mr. Smith?"

"I want you to find something for me."

"What?"

"A body."

There was a gasp from Meat, but he didn't speak. On the tape recorder, Herculeah's mother's voice was as calm as if she were taking statistics.

"Whose body is that?"

"My father's."

"And your father's name? Is it also Smith?"

"No."

"I'll have to have his full name."

There was a pause so long that Herculeah wondered if the tape recorder had stopped on its own. She leaned down and checked. The reel was still turning.

"My father's name is—was Hamilton Crewell."

Meat said, "The Moloch is the old man's son."

Again Herculeah put her finger to her lips.

There was a silence on the tape as well as in the room. Herculeah heard her mother say, "Your father is Hamilton Crewell? I wasn't aware he had a son."

Perhaps the Moloch nodded. There was no sound on the tape.

"When was the last time you saw your father?"

"It was ten years ago."

"Where?"

"In the house. I went there to . . ." another pause,

"see him. I had wanted to go for a long time, but I couldn't get, let us say, out."

"Out?" repeated Herculeah.

"Prison." Meat breathed the word.

Herculeah heard her mother say, "If you are Hamilton Crewell's son, then I would think you stand to inherit a great deal of money." At the same time she heard what sounded like a voice-over. "And just what do you think you're doing?"

This second question did not come from the recorder. It came from the doorway.

Herculeah and Meat looked up. Mrs. Jones was in the door to the hall. She repeated her question, "And just what do you think you're doing?"

Herculeah tried to think of an answer while the tape recorder continued playing. "That's not why I'm here," said the Moloch.

"Why haven't you come forward before this?"

"Let us say, I couldn't."

"Why not?"

Silence.

"What did you mean when you said you couldn't get out?"

In the doorway, Herculeah's mother was holding a rolled sheaf of papers in one hand, a briefcase in the other. She dropped both as she moved quickly over to the desk.

"Have you ever heard of the Bromwell Asylum for the Criminally Insane?"

Herculeah's mother snapped off the recorder before it could play her response. The only sound now was her furious breathing.

"Go home, Meat," she said at last.

"Me?"

"How many people named Meat are there in this house? In this world?"

Herculeah's mother was so mad she was hissing through her teeth now, and a light spray of spit landed on Meat's chin. He did not dare wipe it off because that might offend her and make her even angrier.

He got up clumsily and moved back out of the line of fire. "I was just getting ready to go anyway. But I felt I needed to hear this." He pointed to the hidden recorder. He put one hand to his chin in a thoughtful gesture and wiped off the spit.

"Mrs. Jones," he continued, "the Moloch may be a danger to me. He has seen me several times, and I didn't mean to, but I couldn't help but overhear the words 'criminally insane.' I need to know if the Moloch has any criminally insane plans toward me."

"You don't need to hear anything—not on my tape recorder, you don't. This is extremely confidential material."

Mrs. Jones swirled to point her finger in Herculeah's face. "And you know that, even if Meat doesn't."

Herculeah looked down at the desktop.

Meat cleared his throat. "Well, I'm on my way."

There was a silence as Meat crossed the room. He paused as he passed Mrs. Jones's spilled papers to see if he could see anything. He paused again in the hall to see if he could hear anything.

All he heard was Mrs. Jones saying, "Good-bye, Meat," in such a sharp way that there was only one thing for Meat to do. He left.

17

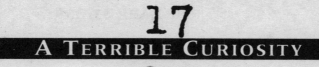

A TERRIBLE CURIOSITY

When the front door had closed behind him, Herculeah's mother said, "What is the explanation for this?"

Herculeah sighed.

"I want the truth."

"Well, yesterday . . ." Herculeah began and, then as if she'd gotten off to a bad start, she began again. "Yesterday, I got a strange sensation in front of Dead Oaks. There was something that I had to know."

She could feel her mother's fury. It was actually heating the air around them. Herculeah pulled at the collar of her sweatshirt.

"When something like this happens, I get this terrible energy. It's like I'll do anything for the truth."

Herculeah still had not looked up to meet her mother's eyes. Her mother's silence was a wall of anger.

"And then, last night, I learned that the Moloch was somehow tied up with the house and—"

"How did you learn that?"

"I saw him there."

"At the house?"

"Yes."

She waited for her mother to question her, to make her tell about those awful moments when she was trapped in the basement, but to Herculeah's relief, her mother said, "Go on."

"Meat saw him too, and we both got—well, it's more than interested."

"Meat was at the Crewell house too?"

Herculeah nodded. "So today I was sitting over there on the sofa, and I had on my glasses—these glasses that help me think—and I remembered your tape recorder.

"Right away I wondered if you'd taped the conversation with the Moloch. And when I found out that you had, Meat and I listened. I knew it wasn't right, but you know I have a terrible curiosity. I got it from you."

"Now, listen to me," her mother said. "The reason I

did not want you to know about this case is because of your 'terrible curiosity,' as you put it. You get into things that don't concern you, and you never stop to think of the danger that might be involved."

"Oh, maybe, every now and then, there's a little danger, but, Mom—"

"This man—Hamilton Crewell's son—has hired me to find his father's body. He is convinced that his father is dead, but he cannot rest easy until the body is found. It's mixed up in his mind—like a dream."

"Where are you going to look?"

"I'm going to start with the house. That's where he thinks the body is."

"Why doesn't he just look himself?"

"I don't know. He's afraid of something."

"What?"

"Something that happened in the house. He wouldn't tell me what. He's a very complicated man."

"Can I go with you?"

"No."

"Mom, I would love it—looking for secret passages and stuff."

"Absolutely not!"

"Why?"

"There's something about this I don't like, Herculeah, something I don't trust."

"What?"

"I don't know myself."

"Because the Moloch was in a mental asylum?" Herculeah asked, then she went on quickly, "I couldn't help but hear that on the tape."

"Don't keep calling him the Moloch. He's William Crewell. Mr. Crewell to you."

"Well, is that what worries you—that he was insane?"

"No, I'm not at all convinced he deserved to be in there. And he has been released from the asylum. I checked on that."

"Then what?"

"I don't know exactly. I found out that he escaped from the asylum twice. The first time he escaped was about ten years ago, and Mr. Crewell was never seen alive after that date."

"And the second time?" Herculeah asked.

"The second time he escaped was . . . sometime in the fall of 1990."

"October fourth," Herculeah said.

"How do you know that?"

"His picture was in the paper the next day," Herculeah said. "Meat and I looked it up in the *Journal*. He was in the crowd of people waiting to see if Hamilton Crewell's body would be brought out of Dead Oaks."

"He really needs to know that his father's dead."

Herculeah touched her glasses on top of her head.

"Mom, when you go in the house, be sure to check the staircase."

"Why?"

"Somebody wrote an anonymous letter to the police. It said there was a body in Dead Oaks, 'down the dark stairs.'"

She broke off. "Mom, please take me with you. You could be in danger. I haven't told you everything I know about this man."

"Then we're even. I haven't told you everything I know either."

18
THE KEY TO DEAD OAKS

"Has your mom gone?" Meat asked.

Herculeah relaxed and shifted the phone to a more comfortable position. "Yes, she's gone, Meat."

"Was she still mad?"

"Not really, but she wasn't happy about us listening to that tape."

"That was obvious."

"She gave me a long, long lecture about it."

"Your mom sort of reminds me of you when she gets mad."

"How?"

"Oh, nothing. Just the way she said, 'How many

people named Meat are there in this house? In this world?' through her teeth."

"I never speak through my teeth."

It sounded to Meat as if Herculeah was getting ready to do it right now. He wanted to add, "But you don't spit on me the way your mom does." However, in her present mood, Herculeah would probably not take that as a compliment. He decided to change the subject.

"Oh, did you get a chance to listen to the rest of the tape?"

"How could I? Mom took it with her. She does not trust me. Oh, I did find out one other thing. She doesn't trust the Moloch either—or Mr. Crewell, as I now have to call him."

"What did she say?"

"Just that the first time he escaped from the asylum was ten years ago, right about the time Hamilton Crewell disappeared, and the second time was seven years later when they went in to find the body. That was when we saw his picture in the paper. He's either incredibly slow or—"

"Did you happen to see those papers your mom dropped on the floor?" Meat interrupted. "Remember, when she saw us listening to the tape, she dropped some papers?"

"I didn't see them."

"They were blueprints, very old blueprints." He paused to let that sink in and then he added, "Probably of Dead Oaks."

"It figures."

"Did she take them with her?"

"Yeah, she wouldn't trust me with anything. Now I'm never going to be able to find out things. She's probably going to get locks."

"I wish I could have seen those blueprints, don't you?"

"Yes, because I think the reason she has those blueprints is to see if there are any hidden places, any passages where Hamilton Crewell could have been when the police came in the house."

"That's what I was thinking." ·

"My mom's probably on her way to the house right now—with the blueprints—going from room to room. I can't stand it!" She broke off, overcome by the desire to be inside the house with her mother. "You want to walk over there?"

"I can't. I promised my mom I wouldn't go near the place. Also, I really do want to stay away from the Moloch."

"He called, did I tell you that?"

"You spoke to him?"

"Yes, it was just for a minute. He left a message for Mom and—"

Herculeah froze.

"What was the message? Herculeah are you still there? Answer me!"

"Oh, it was nothing important. I've got to go, Meat. I'll talk to you later. Bye."

Herculeah continued to sit at the desk for a moment, thinking. Idly she folded her glasses and laid them in front of her on the desk. Then she straightened.

The key, she thought. She leaned forward intently, remembering.

The Moloch's message to her mother had been, "The key is still there."

Herculeah drew in her breath. And without even putting on her glasses to help her think, she knew where the key to Dead Oaks was.

She pushed back the chair and rose.

19
MEAT ON THE MOVE

Meat was standing at his living room window. He had been stationed there ever since his phone conversation with Herculeah.

There had been something about her last words that made him uneasy. "Oh, it was nothing important," she had said. "I've got to go, Meat. I'll talk to you later. Bye."

Something was up, and Meat had been at the window ever since to find out what.

Occasionally he would nervously rub his hands up and down his sweatshirt, and occasionally he would wipe his chin to get off spit that had long been

97

scrubbed away. Indeed his chin was pink from being washed hard. When people spit on you, even by accident, it is hard to wash off.

Meat was rubbing his sweatshirt for the fourth time when the Jones's front door opened and Herculeah appeared.

She had not bothered to put on her jacket, and her hair flew out behind her like a cape. Her hair always seemed to rise, like the hair on a dog's neck, in times of danger, and Meat could see that was what was happening now. His fears rose too.

Herculeah swept her hair behind her, like a gymnast getting an obstacle out of the way.

Meat drew back and rubbed his hands so hard over his shirt that he could feel the electricity.

Herculeah turned in the direction of Dead Oaks. Meat had known all along that was where she was going. He knew, too, that he could not follow.

He sagged against the wall. He was torn between his desire to make sure nothing happened to Herculeah and his promise to his mother that he would not go back to Dead Oaks.

Thirty long minutes passed as he stood there. He was aware that he could be spending his time to more advantage in front of the TV. It was five o'clock, and there was a nature special on the Discovery Channel. Nature specials seemed to soothe Meat, and he needed soothing. Right now he could be watching elephant seals heaving themselves back and forth over the rocks, but he couldn't move.

He sighed so loudly that his mother called from the kitchen, "Are you all right, Albert?"

"Yes, Mom," he called back.

He decided to go to the TV and tape the nature program. That way, when Herculeah returned, he could watch it. He would really need soothing by then.

He was ready to leave the window when he saw the Moloch. Meat pulled back out of sight and peered around the curtains.

The Moloch stopped at Herculeah's house. He glanced both ways to make sure the coast was clear. Then he looked over his shoulder.

Even behind the curtain, Meat knew the exact moment when the Moloch's searing eyes blazed past his house. He felt those eyes had burned a laserlike scar into the vinyl siding.

The Moloch went up the steps and knocked at the door. When there was no answer, he took another glance around and went to the back of the house. He disappeared from view.

Meat stepped closer to the window, but of course it didn't help him see behind the house. He waited nervously, alternately wiping his chin and rubbing his shirt.

When the Moloch reappeared, Meat almost sank to the floor in relief.

The Moloch looked both ways and then, once again, turned in the direction of Dead Oaks.

Meat swallowed loudly, as if he had something in his throat. Then he called, "Mom, I'm going out."

"Not over to Herculeah's."

"I'm not going in the house."

"She's a bad influence."

"I'll be right back."

"Supper's in a half hour."

"I'll be back by then."

"Pork chops."

Meat opened the door and ran across the porch. He went down the stairs holding onto the banister like a small child.

He paused to watch for traffic, even though the street was deserted. He felt the need to take good care of himself. Then he crossed the street and moved quickly to the back of Herculeah's house.

His corduroy pants made a rustling sound as his legs brushed together. Meat had always enjoyed this sound, but now it made him nervous, reminding him that he was moving forward into danger.

He stopped in the backyard. The screen door to the house stood open. This made Meat's heart thud in his chest. The Moloch had gone inside. It looked as if he had just pulled the door open like an unruly child. The latch dangled uselessly against the wood.

Meat walked up the back steps. The smell of the Moloch was in the kitchen. Meat felt sick, but he forced himself to go inside.

He walked to the living room. There was a sheet of paper on the desk. Meat looked down at the big, childish printing.

"I will be there, waiting," he read.

The thought of the Moloch waiting in Dead Oaks made Meat's blood run cold. He was afraid for Herculeah and for Mrs. Jones and, most of all, for himself.

He ran out of the house and down the sidewalk to the corner. He stopped and peered around the side of the insurance building.

The Moloch was almost to the next intersection. He was walking slowly, his shoulders hunched up to meet the brim of his dark hat.

Keeping close to the buildings, Meat moved past the hardware store, the drug store, the dentist that advertised one-day dentures, the card shop . . .

The Moloch turned then, without warning, and Meat ducked into the card shop. His heart was pounding.

"Can I help you?" the clerk asked.

"What?"

"Can I help you find a card?"

"Oh!" He looked around and realized where he was. "Oh, one of these things. A card."

"Yes." The clerk was looking at him strangely.

Meat picked up a Valentine card shaped like a box of candy and raised it so that it shielded his face. With his heart pounding even harder, he moved to the window. He peered over the heart. The Moloch was out of sight.

"Are you looking for something for Valentine's Day?" the clerk asked.

Meat did not care for clerks who tried to sell him things, particularly when he merely needed something to hide behind momentarily. "Not really."

"That's one of our Scratch 'n' Sniff cards. If you scratch it, you can smell chocolate."

"That won't be necessary."

Meat handed the card to the clerk.

"That'll be—" She turned the card over to check the price. "Two dollars and thirty-five cents," she said. When she looked up, Meat was gone.

It was dusk when Herculeah turned the corner onto Antique Row. She drew in a deep breath as she caught sight of Dead Oaks.

The house was dark. The bare trees stood in the overgrown yard like sentries. The wind began to blow, and the limbs rattled. Herculeah wished she had worn a jacket.

Herculeah paused and leaned against the window of Hidden Treasures. She regarded the house. There was no sign that anyone was inside.

She made a quick decision. I'm going to get the key—if it's where I think it is—and I'm going to unlock the door. But I am *not* going inside. I'm going to unlock the door, yell, "Mom, are you in there?" and if she doesn't answer, I'm going home.

Herculeah pulled herself away from the storefront and crossed the street.

She went around the house, up the alley, as she and Meat had done the night before. She stopped at the gate.

Again there was nothing to indicate anyone had come this way. Beyond was the basement door, still half open from her assault. She pushed open the gate and moved into the yard.

At the door to the basement she paused. She felt an unease come over her. She remembered those terrible moments when she had been trapped inside.

She glanced over her shoulder. No one was in sight.

Taking a deep breath, Herculeah reached up as she had seen the Moloch do. It was fortunate that she was tall and could reach above the doorway.

Her fingers found a loose brick, and she removed it. She dropped it behind her with a soft thud. Then, amid the crumbling mortar, she found the key.

For a moment she held it in her hand, looking at it. It was an old key, not one of those modern, sculptured ones. A skeleton key, she thought it was called. The thought caused her to shiver.

THE DARK STAIRS

Clutching the key in her hand, she walked to the side of the house. She hoped this key was to the side door so she wouldn't have to go to the front. She would be seen there.

She walked up the side steps. The concrete had begun to crumble. She crossed the porch and put the key in the lock. She turned.

She heard a click, but the door wouldn't open. It seemed to be swollen shut.

She put her shoulder to it. She shoved with all her might. Then again and again. On the fourth try, the door opened, and her forward drive carried Herculeah into the house.

She had not intended to come inside, but now she already was.

"Mom," she called. "Mom, are you in here?"

There was no answer.

Herculeah was standing in a room as big as the lobby of an old hotel. Her voice seemed to echo through the empty rooms.

There were Persian carpets so thick with dust she could not make out the pattern. Tapestries hung on the walls, and the huge furniture—too big, it seemed for ordinary people—gave Herculeah the feeling she had suddenly become smaller.

She moved a few steps forward to the hallway. She

looked up at the wide marble stairs that led to the upper floor of the house.

"Mom?"

She hesitated. She didn't want to go up the stairs, but something drew her forward.

She started up slowly, almost unwillingly, pulling herself along by the banister.

She heard a rustling noise upstairs.

"Hello," she called.

No answer.

"Is anybody up there?"

I'm just going to take one quick look around, she told herself, and then get out of here. Meat was right. This place is spooky.

And yet she felt a quickening of excitement. She loved moments like this, when she was on the brink of discovery.

At the top of the stairs, she paused. All the doors were closed, and yet she moved instinctively toward the large carved doorway at the front of the hall.

She opened the door and peered inside. This must have been old man Crewell's bedroom. His bed was in the center of a huge, dark rug. Every color was dimmed by the dust.

She moved to the window.

Suddenly something swooped down at Herculeah's

head from the shadows by the closet. She ducked and covered her head with her arms.

Her hair seemed to have gone wild and reached out as if to trap whatever was there. In horror, Herculeah drew her hair closer to her head.

Frantically she turned this way and that, and then she bent double and crouched beside the huge carved bed. Her nose, against the heavy spread, inhaled the dust of years.

She heard the desperate flapping of wings. She peered up through her arms. She saw a mass of black feathers.

"It's a bird," she said aloud. As the creature came to rest, she could see it clearly. "It's a crow!"

She felt weak with relief.

"A crow has somehow gotten in here."

The ordinary nature of the bird made it even better news.

She straightened, and sagged weakly against one of the bed's carved posts.

"A crow!"

She was overcome with relief. She walked to the window and unlocked it. She tried to pull it up. The window, like everything else in this house, hadn't been used in years and wouldn't work. It might as well have been nailed shut.

She began to pull at the window. Her hands were clammy and she dried them on her shirt. The years of hardened paint started to yield.

After one more pull, the paint gave way. She thrust the window up and turned to face the crow.

"It's open now. Come on, crow. Nice crow. See the open window?"

She began to move toward the dresser. "You want to be outside, don't you? You want to be out in the great big world, don't you?"

The crow watched her. Its head was cocked to one side. It paused, and then flapped toward the window. It stopped on the sill.

"That's right," Herculeah said. "Look at that great big wonderful world. Go on! Fly!"

The crow's head bobbed. Then its wings spread and flapped. Herculeah could feel the dusty wind from the sill.

Then the crow lifted its wings, sailed out the window, and swooped across the street.

Herculeah leaned out the window, bracing her elbows on the dusty sill.

"Bye," she said.

Her face grew thoughtful. The bird had to have gotten in somewhere—a chimney, maybe a door left open. She decided to look.

She paused with her elbows on the sill, and she noticed three things:

1. The crow had disappeared.

2. The afternoon air felt wonderfully fresh as she inhaled.

And 3. The Moloch was on the sidewalk below, making his way steadily toward the alley . . . and toward Dead Oaks and her.

21

SOMEBODY'S UPSTAIRS

Herculeah started for the bedroom door. She ran down the hall to the head of the stairs. She had gone down five steps when she heard the Moloch's voice.

"Mrs. Jones?"

He sounded as if he was at the door to the side porch. Herculeah paused with one hand on the banister. For all his slowness, he was already at the door!

"Mrs. Jones?"

This time he sounded as if he was in the living room.

Quietly Herculeah began to back up the five steps. She turned and glanced down the hall. All the doors on the hall were closed except the one to the front bedroom. She couldn't risk opening a door.

Herculeah went back inside. She didn't close the door, because she feared the noise would betray her presence.

She stepped quickly to the window. She looked out. The porch roof was there, and for a moment she considered climbing out on it.

She paused and listened. The Moloch's steps had stopped at the foot of the marble stairway. He was not coming up.

"Mrs. Jones?" he called again. There was something almost like dread in his voice now. "I know somebody's up there."

Herculeah leaned against the marble windowsill and waited. Her eyes moved to a portrait over the old fireplace. She had not noticed it before.

Like everything in the house, it was covered with a layer of dust, but Herculeah could make out the figures of a mother and her son, the child as tall as the mother.

Herculeah moved closer, drawn by something she couldn't explain. Even through the dust, she saw the features of the young boy. She drew in a breath. It was the Moloch.

It wasn't just the size of the boy, it was a certain furtive look in the eyes, the straight mouth that seemed never to have smiled, the hands that hung down as if too heavy to be of any real use.

Herculeah was still staring up at the picture when she heard her mother's voice in the hallway below.

"Mr. Crewell!"

Herculeah started, and then sank against the bed with relief. Instantly she straightened. She didn't want her mother to know she was here. She had to hide.

The window—she would climb out the window. She stopped and shook her head. Her mother would come into the room and slam down the window, and Herculeah would be out on the roof for the rest of her life.

She would have to find some other place. But she wanted to hear the conversation in the hallway below first.

"I thought you were upstairs," the Moloch said.

"No, I just arrived."

"Somebody's upstairs."

"You're imagining things."

"Somebody's upstairs."

"Are you talking about your father?"

Silence.

"I learned this morning," her mother said, "that the reason you were at Bromwell was because you had something to do with your mother's death. Is that correct? Do you remember?"

Silence.

"Your mother died as a result of a fall on the stairs."

In the silence that followed, Herculeah could imagine her mother and the Moloch looking up those long marble stairs together.

"Your father claimed you pushed her."

Then the Moloch spoke. His voice was no longer the deep, frightening voice of a man, but a childlike singsong. "I didn't. I never would. I loved my mother. She was taking me on a trip."

"Where?"

"I don't know. Far away. It was a secret. We couldn't tell anybody."

"Not even your father?"

"Especially not Father."

"And then what?"

"It was night. We got to the head of the stairs. We looked down and Father was in the hallway. He wasn't supposed to be there. He came home early."

"And then?"

"Then my mother said, 'Go to your room, Willie.' That's what she called me. And I always did what she said. I went in my room, but I waited at the door. I knew something bad was going to happen."

"And?" her mother prompted.

"I heard Father saying things to my mother, bad things, and my mother answered, but I couldn't hear what she said. She had a soft voice. Then I heard a scream, a terrible scream."

"Your mother?"

"Yes, and the scream went on and on. I knew she was falling down the steps. I ran out and my mother was lying right there. She didn't move."

"What did your father do?"

"Father pointed his finger at me and screamed, 'You killed her. You killed your mother.'

"I was ten years old, but I was as big and strong as a man, and something snapped in me. I said, 'I did not. I did not kill her.' And I started toward him. I was saying that I hated him and was going to kill him, and I would have. I would have picked him up and thrown him down the stairs, but the servants came out and overcame me."

In the pause that followed, Herculeah heard her mother say quietly, "And your father?"

"Father was like a madman. He kept screaming, 'He killed her. He killed her. He killed his mother. He tried to kill me.'"

There was another silence. Then the Moloch said in a voice so low Herculeah had to move forward to hear him.

"And that's how I came to spend my life in Bromwell Asylum for the Criminally Insane."

22
THE DARK STAIRS

Herculeah heard a shrill whistle from outside. She moved to the open window and glanced out.

Through the dead limbs of the oak tree, she could see Meat across the street. She leaned out and made a shooing motion to get him to go away.

He put one hand behind his ear as if to hear better. She waved him away again. She mouthed the words, "Go away!"

Meat pantomimed the fact that the Moloch was in the house.

Herculeah nodded.

Meat pantomimed the fact that her mother was in there too.

Herculeah would have nodded again, but she heard her mother's voice in the hall below say, "Let's go up there."

"Up the stairs? No."

"Why? If we are ever going to find your father's body, if you are ever going to put your mind at rest, we have to."

"Maybe he's not dead. I heard somebody up there. Maybe I dreamed he was dead. If it's him, he'll say more bad things."

"It's not him."

"Maybe."

"Come with me. I need your help."

"No."

"Your father is dead, isn't he?"

"He should be."

"Then he can't hurt you anymore."

Silence.

"The stairs bother you, don't they? Because of what happened to your mother. Are there other stairs in the house? A lot of these big old houses had stairs for the servants to use."

"Back there."

"Then let's go up that way. You need to face this with me."

At that moment, Herculeah knew that even though the Moloch had not killed his mother, even though he had spent years in an asylum for something he had not done, ten years ago the Moloch had come back here, to this room where she was standing, and had killed his father.

Her eyes darted around the room, taking in the huge carved chest at the foot of the bed: that was big enough to hold a body. But the police had probably checked that. And the huge armoire: that could hold four or five bodies. . . .

She needed to think. She reached into her pocket and took out her glasses. She fastened the slim gold hooks behind her ears. From the street below came another shrill whistle, but Herculeah did not turn around.

She was beginning to get a feeling about what had happened in this room. The Moloch had come to the house—this was his first escape from the asylum. It was probably night. He had gotten the key from over the basement door and unlocked the door to the side porch.

He had come into the darkened living room and into the hallway. He had avoided the marble stairs, even though marble stairs don't give you away by creaking. He had come up the back stairs, down the hall, into this room.

Had he spoken?

Herculeah thought he had, because he had been

waiting for this moment for years, dreaming of it, hoping for it. "I tried to kill you once, and this time I am not going to fail."

Then he had crossed the room. The old man would have come awake by then, perhaps fumbled for the light beside his bed. The Moloch had taken the old man out of the bed, carried him as easily as if he were a doll, and flung him down the stairs. Then he had gone down the back stairs, out of the house. Like a child, reversing his steps, he had put the key back in its hiding place. The next day he was back at the asylum.

But if it had happened that way, the body should have been found at the bottom of the stairs, and the body had never been found. Where was it?

Herculeah broke off her thoughts. She whipped off her glasses. Her mother's voice was in the upstairs hall now.

"That front room, where the door is open, that was your father's room?" she asked.

"Yes."

Herculeah looked around frantically. The door to the dressing room was open. She moved quickly toward it. She slipped inside and flattened herself behind the door.

"You last saw your father here," her mother asked, "in this room?" They were now at the door to the bedroom.

Herculeah felt air on her face. The dressing room window was broken, and dead leaves had blown in through the opening and lay on the tiled floor. The crow had probably gotten in that way.

"I last saw Father at the bottom of the stairs," the Moloch said.

"The marble stairs?" her mother said.

"No."

"The back stairs?"

"No."

Herculeah shoved herself further against the wall, and suddenly she felt herself falling backward. It was as if the wall had collapsed. She struggled to keep her balance.

"Down the dark stairs," the Moloch said.

Herculeah caught herself, but she hung for a moment on the edge of darkness. It was like a bottomless, dark pit, and from this pit came a smell so terrible she felt she would faint.

She gripped the banister. She was at the head of some stairs—a small, private staircase probably used only by one man. She lowered herself to the steps. The door swung shut behind her.

Frozen with shock and growing horror, she could not move for a moment.

She choked. The smell caused tears to pour down her cheeks. Although it was too dark to see, she knew there was a body at the bottom of the stairs.

Then Herculeah did something she had never done before in her life. Herculeah screamed.

23

THE INVESTIGATION

"I came as soon as I could," Meat told everybody in the room. "I would have come sooner except Herculeah leaned out the window and told me not to—well, she didn't tell me, she shooed me like that."

They were gathered in the bedroom of the Crewell house. Herculeah was sitting on the dusty bed. She had stopped screaming, but she held one hand over her nose as if to block out the smell. She was holding her mother's hand.

Her father, who was there in his official capacity, said to Meat, "Do you know anything about this, or are you just curious?"

"Both," Meat answered truthfully.

"Sit down over there."

Chico Jones pointed to a chair on one side of the fireplace. The Moloch was in the chair on the other side. His long arms dangled at his side. He was slumped forward. He still wore his hat, and it shielded his face.

"I'll stand," Meat said. He moved to the opposite side of the room from the Moloch and stood against the wall.

"Now, what happened here?" Chico Jones asked.

"Are you asking me?" Herculeah's mother answered coolly.

"Yes, I am."

"My client, Mr. William Crewell, and I came into the house in an attempt to ascertain what happened to his father." Her mother was speaking with formality.

"You are William Crewell?"

"He is," her mother answered for him.

"Continue."

"We came up the steps, the back ones, crossed the hall, and we heard muffled screaming. Although I had never heard Herculeah scream before, I knew that's who it was.

"The screams seemed to be coming from the dressing room. I rushed in and checked but the room was empty."

"I was behind the door," Herculeah broke in shakily. "I fell through the wall into a secret stairway."

"It wasn't a secret stairway, Herculeah; don't dramatize the incident," her mother said. "It led down to Mr. Crewell's library. A lot of these old houses had multiple stairways. Making service areas—like stairways and closets—look like part of the wall was just a way of making them less noticeable."

"Go on," Chico Jones said.

"We got Herculeah out, and then we noticed that the body of Mr. Crewell, William's father, was lying at the foot of the stairs."

"I could have fallen on him," Herculeah said with a shudder. "That's why I screamed. You'd probably scream too, Dad, if you almost fell on a corpse."

"I hope I never find out," her father said.

The sergeant who was with him, jotting down notes on a clipboard, stifled a smile.

"Apparently," Herculeah's mother continued, "Mr. Crewell fell down the stairs and died there. Whether it was a stroke or an injury or his heart gave out—"

"There could have been some sort of struggle," the sergeant commented. "His cane was up here, and the window was broken as if he'd pulled back to strike someone."

"I think it was a heart attack," Herculeah said.

"We'll leave that to the coroner, shall we?" Chico Jones said.

Herculeah got up, and her mother said quickly, "Are you feeling better?"

"Yes, but I've got to get off this bed."

Her father looked at Herculeah. His stock-in-trade was never letting anyone know what he was thinking, and he was giving her that official look now.

"And what were you doing here?"

"Me? It's a long story."

"We've got all evening."

"Well, I came in and I didn't want to go upstairs, but I did."

"That's the long story?"

"Yes."

"You could be charged with trespassing, you know."

"Dad, you know I didn't mean to trespass."

"She doesn't need to be questioned anymore to-night," her mother said firmly. "She needs to go home and take a shower and go to bed. You can come over tomorrow and get the details. The man's been dead for years. There's no rush."

Herculeah said, "What I don't understand is why the police didn't find him."

"I was here that day," the sergeant said. He took out a stick of gum and folded it into his mouth. "We sure didn't know about that staircase. The note said the body was on the stairway, and we checked both of the ones we knew about." He smiled. "I guess we needed Herculeah's help."

The coroner arrived then, and two attendants came up the stairs with a stretcher.

"The body's in there," Chico Jones told them, "at the bottom of the stairs. If you can find the entrance to the stairs in the library, it might make it easier."

"We'll check it out," the attendant said.

"There'll be an inquest," Chico Jones told them, "after we get the results from the coroner. Mr. Crewell, you'll need to be there for that."

The Moloch nodded his head.

"You too, Mim, Herculeah."

Her mother said, "Of course."

"I can be there too, Lieutenant Jones," Meat said.

"That may not be necessary, Meat."

"I want to know everything that happened."

Herculeah didn't need the inquest or her glasses to know that. She could almost see it.

The Moloch had startled his father in the dressing room. The father had pulled the cane back to strike, breaking the window, but the Moloch had knocked the cane away, picked him up like a toy, and thrown him to his death.

But until the body was found, his father wasn't

really dead. The Moloch couldn't rest. Finally, he'd written that childish note to the police, and come to stand in the crowd, hoping for the end.

"Come on," Herculeah's father was saying.

"We can go?" Herculeah asked, not believing her good luck.

"Yes," her father said, "I'll give you all a ride home." And this time he looked at Herculeah as if she were his daughter, instead of an unfriendly witness.

"Thanks, Dad," she said.

24

HERCULEAH VS THE HYDRA

"So what do you think's going to happen to the Moloch?" Meat asked. Herculeah and Meat were talking on the phone. Herculeah's parents were in the kitchen, having beers and an argument.

"Probably nothing. I don't think they can prove he did it. But you know a funny thing? After you left, he talked to Mom about when he could go back to the asylum. He didn't want to be out in this world. He just wanted to make sure his father was dead. It's sad, really."

"What did your parents say?"

"Nothing about the Moloch, plenty about me."

She heard her father's voice in the kitchen saying, "You cannot let her get involved in your work!"

"I don't let her do anything. You know your daughter better than that!"

"I've got to go," Herculeah said. "My parents are still arguing about me in the kitchen. I want to be in bed before they decide to come in here and argue with me."

Herculeah hung up the phone. She picked up her eyeglasses from the desk. She looked at them for a moment before she hooked the thin metal loops around her ears. The phone rang.

"If that's for me, I'm not here," her mother called.

"Me either," said her father.

Herculeah smiled. They had been saying that every time the phone rang, and every time it had been Meat calling her. She lifted the phone. "Mim Jones's office," she said.

"Channel 16! Channel 16!" Meat's voice said.

"Meat, is it you again?"

"Yes. Turn on Channel 16 quick or you'll miss it!"

"What?" Herculeah removed her glasses, folded them, and set them on the desk.

"They're having something on Channel 16 called *The All-Night Hercules Toga Party*. I just tuned in, and guess what?"

"I can't."

"Hercules vs the Moloch is on TV."

"So what is the Moloch? Have you seen him yet?"

"Yes."

"What is he?"

"A man in a cat mask."

"Meat, be real."

"I am. He's a man in an iron cat mask. I was disappointed too. He's supposed to be a god, and his victims are beautiful girls in short togas—virgins, they call them—and after he ruins the virgins' faces, he says things like, 'Now you are no longer beautiful so you no longer offend me.'"

"Are you making this up?"

"No, I'm watching it as we speak. A boring temple scene's on now. Guys in beards are having veils put on the virgins."

"I cannot believe my mom named me because of a guy in a cat mask. I'm going in the kitchen now and—"

"He's back! He's got a bow and arrow and he's still got on the mask. The big question is what is under the mask. It's like *Phantom of the Opera* where you have to wait till the very end. You want me to tape it for you? So you can see the Moloch's face?"

"Meat, I've seen enough Molochs to last me the rest of my life."

"Actually I have too, but maybe your mom would be interested."

"It would be a big disappointment—a guy in a cat mask. If my mom had seen that, she would have never named me Herculeah. I'd be Trish or Brandi or something."

"You want to stay on the line until the guy takes off his mask? It's probably coming up pretty quick because Hercules is going in the cave."

"No."

"Well, I'll tell you about it tomorrow."

"Good night, Meat."

"Good night."

Herculeah hung up the phone. She picked up the glasses, put them on, and looked through the round circles.

Nothing happened. She had no wonderful thoughts, saw no novels, heard no songs to write, no poems. But, maybe, she thought, the glasses only worked when she needed them—the way they had in Dead Oaks.

The phone rang, and Herculeah picked it up.

"He just took off his mask and guess what?" Meat said.

"Meat, it is almost midnight."

"Look, if you don't want to know what was under

the mask, just say you don't want to know what was under the mask!"

Herculeah weakened. "Oh, all right. What was under the mask?"

"Actually, it wasn't that bad—not bad enough to go around killing virgins over. His face was kind of twisted to the side and red—it was a disappointment if you want the truth." He paused. "But guess what's coming on?"

"I'm too tired."

"Hercules vs the Hydra."

"The Hydra?" Herculeah asked.

"Yes, and I already know what that is—a serpent with nine venomous heads."

"The Hydra," Herculeah said thoughtfully. She had a premonition of something—something in the near future. Herculeah vs the Hydra. The thought made her hair begin to rise. She pulled it back into a ponytail with one hand. Nine heads.

"Want me to tape it?"

"No," she said. "I'll wait for the real thing. Good night again, Meat."

"Good night, Herculeah."

Betsy Byars has written over thirty books for young people, including the Newbery Medal–winner *The Summer of the Swans*. Seven of her novels have been named ALA Notable Books, including *Bingo Brown*, *Gypsy Lover* and *The Burning Questions of Bingo Brown*, which was also a *Booklist* Editor's Choice, "Best of the 80s." Ms. Byars has also received the American Book Award and the Regina Medal, among many other awards and honors.

Betsy Byars lives in Clemson, South Carolina.